P9-DCV-086

Personal Property of
Jaime Rozsnyai

Flora
& Ulysses
The
Illuminated
Adventures

KATE DiCAMILLO

illustrated by K. G. Campbell

CANDLEWICK PRESS

This is a work of fiction. Names, characters, places, and incidents are either products of the author's imagination or, if real, are used fictitiously.

First edition 2013

Library of Congress Catalog Card Number 2012947748
ISBN 978-0-7636-6040-6

14 15 16 17 18 BVG 10 9 8 7 6 5

Printed in Berryville, VA, U.S.A.

This book was typeset in Dante.
The illustrations were created in pencil.

Candlewick Press
99 Dover Street
Somerville, Massachusetts 02144

visit us at www.candlewick.com

For Andrea and Heller, superheroes to me

K. D.

To Dad, who passed it on

K. G. C.

IN THE TICKHAM KITCHEN,
LATE ON A SUMMER AFTERNOON . . .

HAPPY BIRTHDAY TO YOUUUUUU.
WHAT'S THIS, DONALD?
THIS IS YOUR BIRTHDAY PRESENT. IT IS A ULYSSES SUPER-SUCTION, MULTI-TERRAIN 2000X! HAPPY BIRTHDAY.

IT'S A VACUUM CLEANER.

IT'S A ULYSSES 2000X!

YEP, IT'S THE CROWN JEWEL OF VACUUMS. IT FEATURES AN EXTRA-LONG CORD SO THAT ABSOLUTELY NO MESS, NO DIRT, IS EVER OUT OF YOUR REACH.
IT'S INDOOR/OUTDOOR.
IT GOES EVERYWHERE.
IT DOES EVERYTHING!

GOODY.

YOU HAVE TO TRY IT OUT. TURN IT ON!
FOR HEAVEN'S SAKE, DONALD.
PLEASE?

Ulysses 2000X
The World's Great & Lasting Poetry

WHOA.
HEY, NOW.
Ulysses 2000X

Poetry

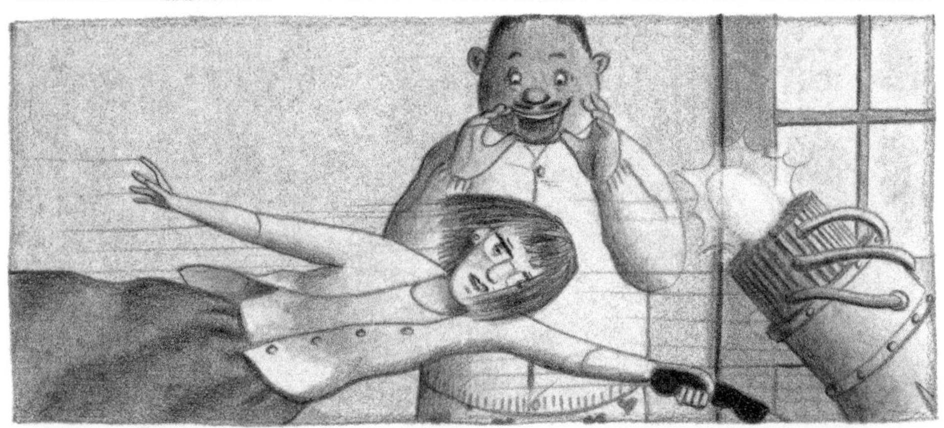

AND THAT'S HOW IT ALL BEGAN.
WITH A VACUUM CLEANER.
REALLY.

CHAPTER ONE
A Natural-Born Cynic

Flora Belle Buckman was in her room at her desk. She was very busy. She was doing two things at once. She was ignoring her mother, and she was also reading a comic book entitled ***The Illuminated Adventures of the Amazing Incandesto!***

"Flora," her mother shouted, "what are you doing up there?"

"I'm reading!" Flora shouted back.

"Remember the contract!" her mother shouted. "Do not forget the contract!"

At the beginning of summer, in a moment of weakness, Flora had made the mistake of signing a contract that said she would "work to turn her face away from the idiotic high jinks of comics and toward the bright light of true literature."

Those were the exact words of the contract. They were her mother's words.

Flora's mother was a writer. She was divorced, and she wrote romance novels.

Talk about idiotic high jinks.

Flora hated romance novels.

In fact, she hated romance.

"I hate romance," said Flora out loud to herself. She liked the way the words sounded. She imagined them floating above her in a comic-strip bubble; it was a comforting thing to have words

hanging over her head. Especially negative words about romance.

Flora's mother had often accused Flora of being a "natural-born cynic."

Flora suspected that this was true.

SHE WAS A NATURAL-BORN CYNIC WHO LIVED IN DEFIANCE OF CONTRACTS!

Yep, thought Flora, *that's me.* She bent her head and went back to reading about the amazing Incandesto.

She was interrupted a few minutes later by a very loud noise.

It sounded as if a jet plane had landed in the Tickhams' backyard.

"What the heck?" said Flora. She got up from her desk and looked out the window and saw Mrs. Tickham running around the backyard with a shiny, oversize vacuum cleaner.

It looked like she was vacuuming the yard.

That can't be, thought Flora. *Who vacuums their yard?*

Actually, it didn't look like Mrs. Tickham knew *what* she was doing.

It was more like the vacuum cleaner was in charge. And the vacuum cleaner seemed to be out of its mind. Or its engine. Or something.

"A few bolts shy of a load," said Flora out loud.

And then she saw that Mrs. Tickham and the vacuum cleaner were headed directly for a squirrel.

"Hey, now," said Flora.

She banged on the window.

"Watch out!" she shouted. "You're going to vacuum up that squirrel!"

She said the words, and then she had a strange moment of seeing them, hanging there over her head.

"YOU'RE GOING TO VACUUM UP THAT SQUIRREL!"

There is just no predicting what kind of sentences you might say, thought Flora. *For instance, who would ever think you would shout, "You're going to vacuum up that squirrel!"?*

It didn't make any difference, though, what words she said. Flora was too far away. The vacuum cleaner was too loud. And also, clearly, it was bent on destruction.

"This malfeasance must be stopped," said Flora in a deep and superheroic voice.

"This malfeasance must be stopped" was what the unassuming janitor Alfred T. Slipper always said before he was transformed into the amazing Incandesto and became a towering, crime-fighting pillar of light.

Unfortunately, Alfred T. Slipper wasn't present.

Terrible Things
CAN HAPPEN TO
YOU!
ILLUMINATED ADVENTURES
AMAZING
INCANDESTO!
Terrible
can happen

Where was Incandesto when you needed him?

Not that Flora really believed in superheroes. But still.

She stood at the window and watched as the squirrel was vacuumed up.

Poof. Fwump.

"Holy bagumba," said Flora.

CHAPTER TWO
The Mind of a Squirrel

Not much goes on in the mind of a squirrel.

Huge portions of what is loosely termed "the squirrel brain" are given over to one thought: food.

The average squirrel cogitation goes something like this: *I wonder what there is to eat.*

This "thought" is then repeated with small variations (e.g., *Where's the food? Man, I sure am hungry. Is that a piece of food?* and *Are there* more *pieces of food?*) some six or seven thousand times a day.

All of this is to say that when the squirrel in the Tickhams' backyard got swallowed up by the Ulysses 2000X, there weren't a lot of terribly profound thoughts going through his head.

As the vacuum cleaner roared toward him, he did not (for instance) think, *Here, at last, is my fate come to meet me!*

He did not think, *Oh, please, give me one more chance and I will be good.*

What he thought was *Man, I sure am hungry.*

And then there was a terrible roar, and he was sucked right off his feet.

At that point, there were no thoughts in his squirrel head, not even thoughts of food.

CHAPTER THREE
The Death of a Squirrel

Seemingly, swallowing a squirrel was a bit much even for the powerful, indomitable, indoor/outdoor Ulysses 2000X. Mrs. Tickham's birthday machine let out an uncertain roar and stuttered to a stop.

Mrs. Tickham bent over and looked down at the vacuum cleaner.

There was a tail sticking out of it.

"For heaven's sake," said Mrs. Tickham, "what next?"

She dropped to her knees and gave the tail a tentative tug.

She stood. She looked around the yard.

"Help," she said. "I think I've killed a squirrel."

CHAPTER FOUR
A Surprisingly Helpful Cynic

Flora ran from her room. She ran down the stairs. As she ran, she thought, *For a cynic, I am a surprisingly helpful person.*

She went out the back door.

Her mother called to her. She said, "Where are you going, Flora Belle?"

Flora didn't answer her. She never answered her mother when she called her Flora Belle.

Sometimes she didn't answer her mother when she called her Flora, either.

Flora ran through the tall grass and cleared the fence between her yard and the Tickhams' in a single bound.

"Move out of the way," said Flora. She gave Mrs. Tickham a shove and grabbed hold of the vacuum cleaner. It was heavy. She picked it up and shook it. Nothing happened. She shook harder. The squirrel dropped out of the vacuum cleaner and landed with a *plop* on the grass.

He didn't look that great.

He was missing a lot of fur. Vacuumed off, Flora assumed.

His eyelids fluttered. His chest rose and fell and rose again. And then it stopped moving altogether.

Flora knelt. She put a finger on the squirrel's chest.

Ulysses
2000X

At the back of each issue of ***The Illuminated Adventures of the Amazing Incandesto!*** there was a series of bonus comics. One of Flora's very favorite bonus comics was entitled *TERRIBLE THINGS CAN HAPPEN TO YOU!* As a cynic, Flora found it wise to be prepared. Who knew what horrible, unpredictable thing would happen next?

TERRIBLE THINGS CAN HAPPEN TO YOU! detailed what action to take if you inadvertently consumed plastic fruit (this happened more often than you would suppose—some plastic fruit was extremely realistic looking); how to perform the Heimlich maneuver on your elderly aunt Edith if she choked on a stringy piece of steak at an all-you-can-eat buffet; what to do if you were wearing a striped shirt and a swarm of locusts descended (run: locusts eat stripes); and, of course, how to administer everyone's favorite lifesaving technique: CPR.

TERRIBLE THINGS CAN HAPPEN TO YOU! did not, however, detail exactly how someone was supposed to give CPR to a squirrel.

"I'll figure it out," said Flora.

"What will you figure out?" said Mrs. Tickham.

Flora didn't answer her. Instead, she bent down and put her mouth on the squirrel's mouth.

It tasted funny.

If she were forced to describe it, she would say that it tasted exactly like squirrel: fuzzy, damp, slightly nutty.

"Have you lost your mind?" said Mrs. Tickham.

Flora ignored her.

She breathed into the squirrel's mouth. She pushed down on his small chest.

She started to count.

CHAPTER FIVE
The Squirrel Obliges

Something strange had happened to the squirrel's brain.

Things had gone blank, black. And then, into this black blankness, there came a light so beautiful, so bright, that the squirrel had to turn away.

A voice spoke to him.

"What's that?" said the squirrel.

The light shone brighter.

The voice spoke again.

"Okay," said the squirrel. "You bet!"

He wasn't sure what, exactly, he was agreeing to, but it didn't matter. He was just so happy. He was floating in a great lake of light, and the voice was singing to him. Oh, it was wonderful. It was the best thing ever.

And then there was a loud noise.

The squirrel heard another voice. This voice was counting. The light receded.

"Breathe!" the new voice shouted.

The squirrel obliged. He took a deep, shuddering breath. And then another. And another.

The squirrel returned.

CHAPTER SIX
In the Event of a Seizure

"Well, he's breathing," said Mrs. Tickham.

"Yes," said Flora. "He is." She felt a swell of pride.

The squirrel rolled over onto his stomach. He raised his head. His eyes were glazed.

"For heaven's sake," said Mrs. Tickham. "Look at him."

She chuckled quietly. She shook her head. And then she laughed out loud. She kept laughing. She laughed and laughed and laughed. She laughed so hard that she started to shake.

Was she having some kind of fit?

Flora tried to remember what ***TERRIBLE THINGS CAN HAPPEN TO YOU!*** advised in the event of a seizure. It had something to do with moving the tongue out of the way or stabilizing it with a stick. Or something.

Flora had saved the squirrel's life; she didn't see any reason she couldn't save Mrs. Tickham's tongue.

The sun sank a little lower in the sky. Mrs. Tickham continued to laugh hysterically.

And Flora Belle Buckman started looking around the Tickhams' backyard for a stick.

CHAPTER SEVEN
The Soul of a Squirrel

The squirrel was a little unsteady on his feet.

His brain felt larger, roomier. It was as if several doors in the dark room of his self (doors he hadn't even known existed) had suddenly been flung wide.

Everything was shot through with meaning, purpose, light.

However, the squirrel was still a squirrel.

And he was hungry. Very.

WHO CAN SAY WHAT ASTONISHMENTS ARE HIDDEN INSIDE THE MOST MUNDANE BEING?
Ulysses 2000X

CHAPTER EIGHT
Helpful Information

Flora and Mrs. Tickham noticed at the same time.

"The squirrel," said Flora.

"The vacuum cleaner," said Mrs. Tickham.

Together, they stared at the Ulysses 2000X and at the squirrel, who was holding it over his head with one paw.

"That can't be," said Mrs. Tickham.

The squirrel shook the vacuum cleaner.

"That can't be," said Mrs. Tickham.

"You already said that," said Flora.

"I'm repeating myself?"

"You're repeating yourself."

"Maybe I have a brain tumor," said Mrs. Tickham.

It was certainly possible that Mrs. Tickham had a brain tumor. Flora knew from reading ***TERRIBLE THINGS CAN HAPPEN TO YOU!*** that a surprising number of people were walking around with tumors in their brains and didn't even know it. That was the thing about tragedy. It was just sitting there, keeping you company, waiting. And you had absolutely no idea.

This was the kind of helpful information you could get from the comics if you paid attention.

The other kind of information that you absorbed from

the regular reading of comics (most particularly from the regular reading of *The Illuminated Adventures of the Amazing Incandesto!*) was that impossible things happened all the time.

For instance, heroes—superheroes—were born of ridiculous and unlikely circumstances: spider bites, chemical spills, planetary dislocation, and, in the case of Alfred T. Slipper, from accidental submersion in an industrial-size vat of cleaning solution called Incandesto! (The Cleaning Professional's Hardworking Friend).

"I don't think you have a brain tumor," said Flora. "There might be another explanation."

"Uh-huh," said Mrs. Tickham. "What's the other explanation?"

"Have you ever heard of Incandesto?"

"What?" said Mrs. Tickham.

"Who," said Flora. "Incandesto is a who. He's a superhero."

"Right," said Mrs. Tickham. "And your point is?"

Flora raised her right hand. She pointed with a single finger at the squirrel.

"Surely you're not implying . . ." said Mrs. Tickham.

The squirrel lowered the vacuum cleaner to the ground. He held himself very still. He considered both of them. His whiskers twitched and trembled. There were cracker crumbs on his head.

He was a squirrel.

Could he be a superhero, too? Alfred T. Slipper was a janitor. Most of the time, people looked right past him. Sometimes (often, in fact) they treated him with disdain. They had no idea of the astonishing acts of heroism, the blinding light, contained within his outward, humdrum disguise.

Only Alfred's parakeet, Dolores, knew who he was and what he could do.

"The world will misunderstand him," said Flora.

"You bet it will," said Mrs. Tickham.

"Tootie?" shouted Mr. Tickham from the back door. "Tootie, I'm hungry!"

Tootie?

What a ridiculous name.

Flora couldn't resist the urge to say it out loud. "Tootie," she said. "Tootie Tickham. Listen, Tootie. Go inside. Feed your husband. Say nothing to him or to anyone else about any of this."

"Right," said Tootie. "Say nothing. Feed my husband. Okay, right." She began walking slowly toward the house.

Mr. Tickham called out, "Are you done vacuuming? What about the Ulysses? Are you just going to leave it sitting there?"

"Ulysses," whispered Flora. She felt a shiver run from the back of her head to the base of her spine. She might be a natural-born cynic, but she knew the right word when she heard it.

"Ulysses," she said again.

She bent down and held out her hand to the squirrel.

"Come here, Ulysses," she said.

CHAPTER NINE
The Whole World on Fire

She spoke to him.

And he understood her.

What the girl said was "Ulysses. Come here, Ulysses."

And without thinking, he moved toward her.

"It's okay," she said.

And he believed her. It was astonishing. Everything was astonishing. The setting sun was illuminating each blade of grass. It was reflecting off the girl's glasses, making a halo of light around the girl's round head, setting the whole world on fire.

The squirrel thought, *When did things become so beautiful? And if it has been this way all along, how is it that I never noticed before?*

"Listen to me," the girl said. "My name is Flora. Your name is Ulysses."

Okay, thought the squirrel.

She put her hand on him. She picked him up. She cradled him in her left arm.

He felt nothing but happiness. Why had he always been so terrified of humans? He couldn't imagine.

Actually, he could imagine.

There had been that time with the boy and the BB gun.

There had, truthfully, been a lot of incidents with humans (some involving BB guns, some not), and all of them had been violent, terrifying, and soul-destroying.

But this was a new life! And he was a changed squirrel.

He felt spectacular. Strong, smart, capable—and also: hungry.

He was very, very hungry.

CHAPTER TEN
Squirrel Smuggling

Flora's mother was in the kitchen. She was typing. She wrote on an old typewriter, and when she pounded the keys, the kitchen table shook and the plates on the shelves rattled and the silverware in the drawers cried out in a metallic kind of alarm.

Flora had decided that this was part of the reason her parents had divorced. Not the noise of the writing, but the writing itself. Specifically, the writing of romance.

Flora's father had said, "I think that your mother is so in love with her books about love that she doesn't love me anymore."

And her mother had said, "Ha! Your father is so far off in left field that he wouldn't recognize love if it stood up in his soup and sang."

Flora had a hard time imagining what love would be doing standing in a bowl of soup and singing, but these were the kind of idiotic words her parents spoke. And they said the words to each other, even though they were pretending that they were talking to Flora.

It was all very annoying.

"What are you doing?" her mother said to Flora. She was sucking on a Pitzer Pop. It made her words sound rocky and sharp-edged. Her mother used to smoke and then she stopped, but she still had to have something in her mouth when she typed, so she consumed a lot of Pitzer Pops. This one was orange flavored. Flora could smell it.

"Oh, nothing," said Flora. She glanced at the squirrel in her arms.

"Good," said her mother. She whacked the carriage return on the typewriter without looking up. She kept typing. "Are you still standing there?" her mother said. She typed some more words. She hit the carriage return again. "I'm on a deadline here. It's hard to concentrate with you standing over me breathing like that."

"I could stop breathing," said Flora.

"Oh, don't be ridiculous," said her mother. "Go upstairs and wash your hands. We're going to eat soon."

"Okay," said Flora. She walked past her mother and into the living room, still carrying Ulysses in the crook of her arm. It didn't seem possible, but it was true. She had smuggled a squirrel into the house. And she had done it right under her mother's nose. Or behind her back. Or something.

In the living room, at the base of the stairs, the little shepherdess lamp was waiting, a pink-cheeked smirk plastered on her face.

Flora hated the little shepherdess.

Her mother had bought the lamp with her first royalty check from her first book, *On Feathered Wings of Joy,* which was the stupidest title for a book that Flora had ever heard in her life.

Her mother had sent away to London for the lamp. When it arrived, she unpacked it and plugged it in, and then she clapped her hands and said, "Oh, she's so beautiful. Isn't she beautiful? I love her with all my heart."

Flora's mother never called Flora beautiful. She never said that she loved *her* with all her heart. Luckily, Flora was a cynic and didn't care whether her mother loved her or not.

"I think that I will call her Mary Ann," her mother had said.

"Mary Ann?" said Flora. "You're going to name a lamp?"

"Mary Ann, shepherdess to the lost," said her mother.

"Who's lost, exactly?" said Flora.

But her mother hadn't bothered to answer that question.

"This," Flora said to the squirrel, "is the little shepherdess. Her name is Mary Ann. Unfortunately, she lives here, too."

The squirrel considered Mary Ann.

Flora narrowed her eyes and stared at the lamp.

She knew that it was ridiculous, but sometimes she felt as if Mary Ann knew something that she didn't know, that the little shepherdess was keeping some dark and terrible secret.

"You stupid lamp," said Flora. "Mind your own business. Mind your sheep."

Actually, there was just one sheep, a tiny lamb curled up at Mary Ann's pink-slippered feet. Flora always wanted to say to the little shepherdess, "If you're such a great shepherdess, where are the rest of your sheep, huh?"

"We can just ignore her," said Flora to Ulysses.

She turned away from the smug and glowing Mary Ann and climbed the stairs to her room, holding Ulysses gently, carefully in her arms.

He didn't glow, but he was surprisingly warm for someone so small.

CHAPTER ELEVEN
A Gigantic Vat of Incandesto!

She put Ulysses down on her bed, and he looked even smaller sitting there in the bright overhead light.

He also looked pretty bald.

"Good grief," said Flora.

The squirrel certainly didn't look very heroic. But then, neither did the nearsighted, unassuming janitor Alfred T. Slipper.

Ulysses looked up at Flora, and then he looked down at his tail. He seemed relieved to see it. He lowered his nose and sniffed along the length of it.

"I'm hoping that you can understand me," said Flora.

The squirrel raised his head. He stared at her.

"Wow," said Flora. "Great, okay. I can't understand you. And that's a small problem. But we'll figure out a way to communicate, okay? Nod at me if you understand what I'm saying. Like this."

Flora nodded.

And Ulysses nodded back.

Flora's heart leaped up high in her chest.

"I'm going to try and explain what happened to you, okay?"

Ulysses nodded his head very fast.

And again, Flora's heart leaped up high inside of her in a hopeful and extremely uncynical kind of way. She closed her eyes. *Don't hope,* she told her heart. *Do not hope; instead, observe.*

"Do not hope; instead, observe" was a piece of advice that appeared often in ***TERRIBLE THINGS CAN HAPPEN TO YOU!*** According to ***TERRIBLE THINGS!,*** hope sometimes got in the way of action. For instance, if you looked at your elderly aunt Edith choking on a piece of steak from the all-you-can-eat buffet and you told yourself, *Man, I sure hope she's not choking,* you would waste several valuable lifesaving, Heimlich maneuver–performing seconds.

"Do not hope; instead, observe" were words that Flora, as a cynic, had found useful in the extreme. She repeated them to herself a lot.

"Okay," said Flora. She opened her eyes. She looked at the squirrel. "What happened is that you got vacuumed. And because you got vacuumed, you might have, um, powers."

Ulysses gave her a questioning look.

"Do you know what a superhero is?"

The squirrel continued to stare at her.

"Right," said Flora. "Of course you don't. A superhero is someone with special powers, and he uses those powers to fight the forces of darkness and evil. Like Alfred T. Slipper, who is also Incandesto."

Ulysses blinked several times in a nervous kind of way.

AND NOW TO THE VAT OF INCANDESTO!
INCANDESTO
I'M SICK OF S
YOU MOPE ARO
WITH THAT MOP!
PAXATAWKET
Life Insurance
Where Every Life Counts
AND THEN HE TOLD ME TO "MOP HAPPY" OR NOT MOP AT ALL.

"Look," said Flora. She grabbed ***The Illuminated Adventures of the Amazing Incandesto!*** off her desk. She pointed at Alfred in his janitor uniform.

"See?" she said. "This is Alfred, and he is an unassuming, nearsighted, stuttering janitor who works cleaning the multifloor offices of the Paxatawket Life Insurance Company. He lives a quiet life in his studio apartment with only his parakeet, Dolores, for company."

Ulysses looked down at the picture of Alfred and then up at Flora.

"Okay," said Flora. "So, one day Alfred takes a tour of the Incandesto! cleaning solution factory, and he slips (Alfred T. *Slipper*—get it?) into a gigantic vat of Incandesto! and it changes him. And so now, when there is a great crisis, when malfeasance is apparent, Alfred turns himself into . . ." Flora flipped through the pages of the comic and stopped at the panel that showed the glowing, powerful Incandesto.

"Incandesto!" she said. "See? Alfred T. Slipper becomes a righteous pillar of light so painfully bright that the most heinous villain trembles before him and confesses!"

Flora realized that she was shouting the tiniest bit.

She looked down at Ulysses. His eyes were enormous in his small face.

Flora tried to sound calm, reasonable. She lowered her voice. "As Incandesto," she said, "Alfred sheds light into the darkest corners of the universe. He can fly. Also, he visits the elderly. And that's what a superhero is. And I think you might be one, too. At least, I think you have powers. So far, all we know about you is that you're really strong."

Ulysses nodded. He puffed out his chest.

"Flora!" her mother shouted. "Get down here. Dinner is ready."

"But what else can you do?" said Flora to the squirrel. "And if you truly are a superhero, how will you fight evil?"

Ulysses furrowed his brow.

Flora bent down. She put her face close to his. "Think about it," she said. "Imagine what we might be able to do."

"Flora Belle!" her mother shouted. "I can hear you up there talking to yourself. You shouldn't talk to yourself. People will hear you and think that you're strange."

"I'm not talking to myself!" Flora shouted.

"Well, then, with whom are you speaking?"

"A squirrel!"

There was a long silence from down below.

And then her mother shouted, "That's not funny, Flora Belle. Get down here right now!"

CHAPTER TWELVE
The Forces of Evil

When Flora came back upstairs after dinner, she found Ulysses curled up in a tight little ball, sleeping on her pillow. She put out her hand and touched his forehead with one finger.

His eyes twitched, but they didn't open.

She picked up the pillow and moved it carefully to the foot of the bed. She changed into her pajamas, lay down, and imagined the words

A SUPERHERO SQUIRREL RESTED AT HER FEET,
AND SO SHE WAS NOT LONELY AT ALL

emblazoned on the ceiling above her.

"That's exactly right," she said.

Before the divorce, before her father had moved out of the house and into an apartment, he had often sat beside her at night and read aloud to her from ***The Illuminated Adventures of the Amazing Incandesto!*** It was his favorite comic. It always cheered him up to read about Alfred T. Slipper and Dolores. Her father did an excellent parakeet imitation. "Holy bagumba!" he would say in the voice of Dolores. "Holy unanticipated occurrences!"

"Holy unanticipated occurrences!" was what Dolores would say when something truly unexpected and unbelievable was happening, which was basically all the time. Life was pretty exciting when you were Incandesto's parakeet.

Flora sat up and looked down at the sleeping squirrel.

"Holy unanticipated occurrences!" she said.

It sounded better when her father said it.

Not that he said it these days. He didn't say much of anything anymore. Her father had always been a sad, quiet man, but since the divorce, he had become even sadder and quieter. Which was fine with Flora. Really. Cynics don't like a lot of chatter.

Besides, Alfred T. Slipper was a quiet man, too. For instance, when he was on his tour of the Incandesto! manufacturing facility and had fallen into the vat of Incandesto!, he hadn't said a single word. Not even "oops."

Words had appeared above his head, however, and Flora's father had read those words to her so many times that she could recite them by heart:

HE IS AN UNASSUMING JANITOR. BUT HE WILL DARE TO BATTLE THE DARKNESS OF THE UNIVERSE. DO YOU DOUBT HIM? DO NOT. ALFRED T. SLIPPER WILL LIVE TO FIGHT THE FORCES OF EVIL. HE WILL BECOME KNOWN TO THE WORLD AS INCANDESTO!

Flora lay back down. *If the squirrel were in a comic,* she thought, *what words would have appeared in the space over his head when he was sucked into the vacuum cleaner?*

HE IS AN UNASSUMING SQUIRREL.

Yep.

BUT HE WILL SOON CONQUER VILLAINS OF ALL STRIPES. HE WILL DEFEND THE DEFENSELESS AND PROTECT THE WEAK.

That sounded good, too.

HE WILL BECOME KNOWN TO THE WORLD AS ULYSSES!

Holy bagumba! Anything could happen. Together, she and Ulysses could change the world. Or something.

"Do not hope; instead, observe," Flora whispered to calm herself down. "Just observe the squirrel."

And then she fell asleep.

CHAPTER THIRTEEN
The Typewriter

He woke in darkness. His heart was beating very fast. Something had happened. What was it?

He couldn't think.

He was too hungry to think.

He sat up and looked around the room. He was in bed, and Flora's feet were in his face. She was snoring. He could see the outline of her round head. He loved that head.

But, man, he was hungry.

The door to the bedroom was open. Ulysses got off the pillow and went out of the room. He crept along the dark hallway. He went down the stairs and past the little shepherdess.

The house was dark, but there was a light on in the kitchen.

The kitchen!

That was exactly where he needed to be.

He put his nose up. He sniffed. He smelled something cheesy, wonderful. He ran through the living room and the dining room and into the kitchen. He climbed up on the counter. And there it was! A lone cheese puff, perched on the edge of the red Formica countertop. He ate it. It was delicious.

Maybe there were more cheese puffs.

He opened a cabinet. And, yes, there was a big bag with the

beautiful word *Cheese-o-mania* written in golden script on the front of it.

He ate until the bag was empty. And then he burped softly, gratefully. He looked around the kitchen.

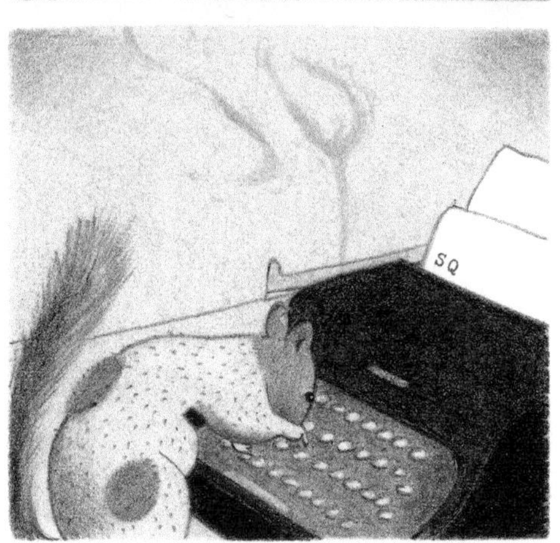

IN THE DARKENED KITCHEN,
THE UNASSUMING SQUIRREL WORKED SLOWLY.

HIS WHISKERS TREMBLED. HIS HEART SANG.

WAS HE FIGHTING EVIL?

WHO COULD SAY?

CHAPTER FOURTEEN
Squirtel!

"Flora Belle Buckman! Get down here right now!"

"Don't call me Flora Belle," Flora muttered. She opened her eyes.

The room was bright with sunlight. She had been dreaming something wonderful. What was it?

She had been dreaming about a squirrel. In her dream, he was flying with his legs straight out in front of him and his tail straight out behind him. He was a squirrel on his way to save someone! He looked supremely, magnificently heroic.

Flora sat up and looked down at her feet. There was Ulysses, sleeping on the pillow. And he did look heroic. In fact, he was glowing. Just like Incandesto! Except oranger. He was extremely orange.

"What the heck?" said Flora.

She leaned over Ulysses and reached out a finger to touch his ear. She held the finger up to the light. Cheese. He was covered in cheese dust.

"Uh-oh," said Flora.

"Flora!" her mother shouted. "I'm not kidding. Get down here right now!"

Flora went down the stairs and past Mary Ann, whose cheeks were glowing a healthy and disgusting pink.

"You stupid lamp," said Flora.

"Now!" shouted Flora's mother.

Flora broke into a trot.

She found her mother standing in the kitchen in her bathrobe, staring at the typewriter.

"What's this?" her mother said. She pointed at the typewriter.

"That's your typewriter," said Flora.

She knew that her mother was absentminded and preoccupied, but this was ridiculous. How could she not recognize her own typewriter?

"I know it's my typewriter," said her mother. "I'm talking about the piece of paper in it. I'm talking about the words on the paper."

Flora leaned forward. She squinted. She tried to make sense of the word typed at the top of the page.

Squirtel!

"Squirtel!" said Flora out loud; she felt a surge of delight at the zippy idiocy of the word. It was almost as good a word as *Tootie.*

"Keep reading," said her mother.

"'Squirtel!'" said Flora again. "'I am. Ulysses. Born anew.'"

"Do you think that's funny?" said her mother.

"Not really," said Flora. Her heart was beating very fast in her chest. She felt dizzy.

"I have told you and told you to leave this typewriter alone," said her mother.

"I didn't . . ." said Flora.

"What goes on here is a serious business," said her mother. "I am a professional writer. I am under deadline for this novel. This is no time for high jinks. Plus, you ate a whole bag of cheese puffs."

"I did not," said Flora.

Her mother pointed at an empty Cheese-o-mania bag on the counter. And then she pointed at the typewriter.

Flora's mother liked to point at things.

"You left cheese dust all over the typewriter. That's disrespectful. And you simply cannot eat a whole bag of cheese puffs. It's not healthy. You'll become stout."

"I didn't . . ." said Flora.

But then another wave of dizziness came over her.

The squirrel could type!

Holy unanticipated occurrences!

"I'm sorry," said Flora in a small voice.

"Well," said her mother. She raised her finger. She was obviously getting ready to point at something again.

Fortunately, the doorbell rang.

CHAPTER FIFTEEN
The Electric Chair

To say that the Buckman doorbell "rang" would be inaccurate.

Something had happened to the bell; its inner workings had become twisted, warped, confused, so that instead of emitting a pleasant *ding* or *bong,* the doorbell now sent an angry, window-shattering, you-guessed-the-wrong-answer-on-a-game-show kind of buzz through the Buckman house.

To Flora, the doorbell sounded like the electric chair.

Not that she had ever heard an electric chair, but she had read about electric chairs in ***TERRIBLE THINGS CAN HAPPEN TO YOU!*** That particular installment of the comic had not contained any advice other than that it would be best to avoid getting to a place in your life where you might have to face the electric chair and any noises it was capable of making. Flora had found it to be a vaguely threatening and not at all useful issue of ***TERRIBLE THINGS!***

"That's your father," said Flora's mother. "He rings that doorbell to make me feel guilty."

The doorbell buzzed and crackled again.

"See?" said her mother.

Flora didn't see.

How could one person ringing a doorbell make another person feel guilty?

It was ridiculous.

But then, just about everything that Flora's mother said or wrote sounded faintly ridiculous to Flora. For example: *On Feathered Wings of Joy.* Since when did joy have feathered wings?

"Don't just stand there, Flora Belle. Go open the door. Let him in. He's *your* father. He's here to see you. Not me."

The electric-chair knell of the doorbell sounded through the house again.

"For the love of Pete!" said her mother. "What's he doing? Leaning on the thing? Go let him in, would you?"

Flora walked slowly through the dining room and into the living room. She shook her head in amazement.

Upstairs, in her room, there was a squirrel who could lift a vacuum cleaner over his head with one paw.

Upstairs, in her room, there was a squirrel who could *type.*

Holy bagumba, thought Flora. *Things are going to change around here. We're going to be vanquishing villains left and right.* She smiled a very large smile.

The doorbell gave another outraged sizzle.

Flora was still smiling when she unlocked the door and opened it wide.

CHAPTER SIXTEEN
Victims of Extended Hallucinations

It was not her father at the door.

It was Tootie.

"Tootie Tickham!" said Flora.

Tootie stepped through the door and into the living room, and then she stopped. Her eyes widened. "What in the world?" she said.

Flora didn't even bother turning around. She knew what Tootie was looking at.

"That's the little shepherdess," said Flora. "The guardian of lost sheep and light. Or something. She belongs to my mother."

"Right," said Tootie. She shook her head. "Well, never mind about the lamp." She took another step closer to Flora. "Where's the squirrel?" she whispered.

"Upstairs," Flora whispered back.

"I've come to check and see if what I think happened yesterday actually happened, or if I'm the victim of an extended hallucination."

Flora looked Tootie in the eye. She said, "Ulysses can type."

"Who can type?" said Tootie.

"The squirrel. He's a superhero."

Tootie said, "For heaven's sake, what kind of superhero types?"

It was a good (and also slightly disturbing) point. How, exactly, was a typing squirrel going to fight villains and change the world?

"George?" shouted Flora's mother.

"It's not Pop!" Flora shouted back. "It's Mrs. Tickham."

There was a silence from the kitchen, and then Flora's mother came into the living room with a big, fake adult smile plastered on her face. "Mrs. Tickham," she said. "What a lovely surprise. What can we do for you?"

Tootie smiled a big, fake adult smile back. "Oh," she said. "I just came to pay Flora a visit."

"Who?"

"Flora," said Tootie. "Your daughter."

"Really?" said Flora's mother. "You came to see Flora?"

"I'll be right back," said Flora.

She ran out of the living room and through the dining room.

"What a truly extraordinary lamp," she heard Tootie say.

"Oh, do you like it?" said Flora's mother.

Ha! thought Flora.

And then she was out of the dining room and into the kitchen. She ripped the paper out of the typewriter and looked down at the words; they were absolutely not a hallucination.

"Holy bagumba," said Flora.

A loud scream echoed through the house.

Flora took the paper and shoved it down the front of her pajamas and ran back into the living room.

Ulysses was sitting on top of Mary Ann.

Or rather, he was trying to sit on top of Mary Ann.

His feet were scrabbling to gain purchase on the little shepherdess's pink-flowered lampshade. He paused in his efforts and looked at Flora in an apologetic and hopeful way, and then he returned to wobbling back and forth.

"Oh, my goodness," said Tootie.

"How did it get in here?" shouted Flora's mother. "It just came flying down the stairs."

"Yes," said Tootie. She gave Flora a meaningful look. "*Flying.*"

"It absolutely scared the living daylights out of me and Mrs. Tickham. We screamed."

"We did," said Tootie. "We screamed. There's just no end to the excitement."

"If that squirrel breaks my lamp, I don't know what I'll do. Mary Ann is very precious to me."

"Mary Ann?" said Tootie.

"I'll just get him off the lamp, okay?" said Flora. She put out a hand.

"Don't touch it!" screamed her mother. "It has a disease."

The doorbell, as if it were echoing Flora's mother's advice, buzzed its terrible warning buzz.

Flora and her mother and Tootie all turned.

A small voice called out.

The voice said, "Great-Aunt Tootie?"

CHAPTER SEVENTEEN
I Smell Squirrel

There was a boy at the door.

He was short, and his hair was so blond that it looked almost white. His eyes were hidden behind enormous dark glasses.

In addition to ***TERRIBLE THINGS CAN HAPPEN TO YOU!, The Illuminated Adventures of the Amazing Incandesto!*** regularly featured a second bonus comic entitled ***The Criminal Element Is Among Us. The Criminal Element*** gave very specific pointers on how to never, ever be fooled by a criminal, and one of the oft-repeated dictums of ***The Criminal Element*** was that the best way to get to know a person was to look him or her directly in the eye.

Flora tried to look the boy in the eye, but all she saw was a reflection of herself in his dark glasses.

She looked short and uncertain, like an accordion in pajamas.

"William," said Tootie, "I told you to stay put."

"I heard screaming," said the boy. His voice was high and thin. "I was concerned. I came as fast as I could. Unfortunately, on the way over here, I had a small but extremely violent encounter with some variety of shrub. And now I'm bleeding.

I think I'm bleeding. I'm pretty sure I smell blood. But no one should be concerned. Please, don't overreact."

"This," said Tootie, "is my nephew."

"Great-nephew," said the boy. "And I hope I don't need stitches. Do you think I need stitches?"

"His name is William," said Tootie.

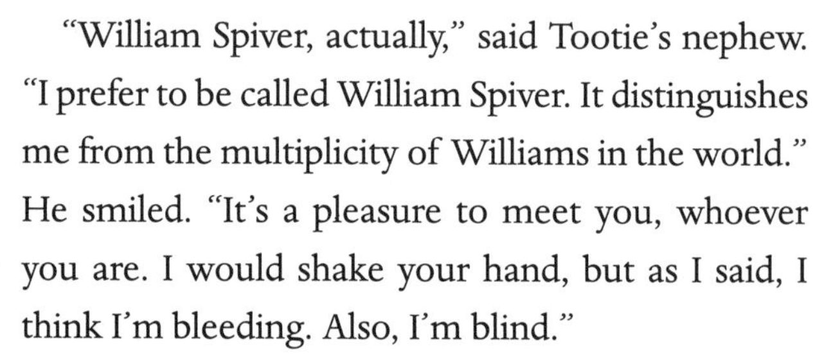

"William Spiver, actually," said Tootie's nephew. "I prefer to be called William Spiver. It distinguishes me from the multiplicity of Williams in the world." He smiled. "It's a pleasure to meet you, whoever you are. I would shake your hand, but as I said, I think I'm bleeding. Also, I'm blind."

"You are not blind," said Tootie.

"I am suffering from a temporary blindness induced by trauma," said William Spiver.

Temporary blindness induced by trauma.

The words sent a chill down Flora's spine.

Seemingly, there was no end to the things that could go wrong with human beings. Why hadn't ***TERRIBLE THINGS CAN HAPPEN TO YOU!*** done an issue on temporary blindness induced by trauma? Or, for that matter, one on extended hallucinations?

"I am temporarily blind," said William Spiver again.

"How unfortunate," said Flora's mother.

"He's not blind," said Tootie. "But as of this morning, he is staying with me for the summer. Imagine my surprise and excitement."

"I have nowhere else to go, Great-Aunt Tootie," said William Spiver. "You know that. I am at the mercy of the winds of fate."

"Oh," said Flora's mother. She clapped her hands. "How wonderful. A little friend for Flora."

"I don't need a little friend," said Flora.

"Of course you do," said her mother. She turned to Tootie. "Flora is very lonely. She spends far too much time reading comics. I've tried to break her of the habit, but I'm very busy with my novel writing and she is alone a lot. I'm worried that it has made her strange."

"I'm not strange," said Flora. This seemed like a safe statement to make when someone as truly, profoundly strange as William Spiver was standing beside her.

"I would be happy to be your friend," said William Spiver. "Honored." He bowed.

"How lovely," said Flora's mother.

"Yes," said Flora. "How lovely."

"The blind," said William Spiver, "even the temporarily blind, have an excellent sense of smell."

"Oh, for heaven's sake," said Tootie. "Here we go."

"I have to tell you that I smell something out of the

ordinary, something that is not usually smelled within the confines of the human domestic sphere," said William Spiver. He cleared his throat. "I smell squirrel."

Squirrel!

Confronted with the spectacle of William Spiver, they had forgotten about Ulysses.

Flora and her mother and Tootie all turned and looked at Ulysses. He was still on top of Mary Ann. He had managed to balance himself on the small blue-and-green globe that was at the center of the lampshade.

"That squirrel," said Flora's mother. "He's rabid, diseased. He's got to go."

CHAPTER EIGHTEEN
A Scientific Adventure

"Why don't you let me take the squirrel?" Tootie said to Flora's mother. "I'll just return him to the wild."

"If you can call the backyard the wild," said William Spiver.

"Hush up, William," said Tootie. She reached out for Ulysses.

"Don't touch it!" shrieked Flora's mother. "Not without gloves. It has some sort of disease."

"If you could just get me some gloves, then," said Tootie, "I'll pluck the squirrel off the lampshade and whisk him out of here and set him free. The kids can come along. It will be a scientific adventure."

"It doesn't sound very scientific to me," said William Spiver.

"Well," said Flora's mother, "I don't know. Flora Belle's father is coming to pick her up for their Saturday visit. He'll be here any minute now. And she's still in her pajamas."

"Flora Belle?" said William Spiver. "What a lovely, melodious name."

"It will all take just a minute," said Tootie in a low, soothing voice. "The kids can get to know each other."

"I'll get you some gloves," said Flora's mother.

And so now here they were, walking over to Tootie's, getting to know each other. Or something.

Tootie had on a pair of dishwashing gloves that went all the way up to her elbows. The gloves were bright pink, and they glowed in a cheery, radioactive sort of way.

In Tootie's gloved hands was Ulysses. Behind Tootie was Flora.

And next to Flora was William Spiver. His left hand rested on her shoulder.

"Do you mind, Flora Belle?" he had said. "Would it trouble you terribly if I put my hand on your shoulder and allowed you to guide me back to Great-Aunt Tootie's house? The world is a treacherous place when you can't see."

Flora didn't bother pointing out to him that the world was a treacherous place when you *could* see.

And speaking of treacherousness, things were not, in any way, progressing as Flora had planned. She had envisioned Ulysses fighting crime, criminals, villainy, darkness, treachery; she had imagined him flying (holy bagumba!) through the world with her (Flora Buckman!) at his side. Instead, here she was leading a temporarily blind boy through her own backyard. It was anticlimactic, to say the least.

"Have you released the squirrel yet, Great-Aunt Tootie?"

"No," said Tootie, "I have not."

"Why do I sense that there is more going on here than meets the eye?" said William Spiver.

"Just keep quiet until we get back to the house, William," said Tootie. "Can you do that? Keep quiet for a minute?"

"Of course I can," said William Spiver. He sighed. "I'm an old pro at keeping quiet."

Flora doubted, very much, that this was true.

William Spiver squeezed her shoulder. "May I inquire how old you are, Flora Belle?"

"Don't squeeze my shoulder. I'm ten."

"I am eleven years old," said William Spiver. "Which surprises me, I must say. I feel much, much older than eleven. Also, I know for a fact that I am smaller than your average eleven-year-old. It may even be that I'm shrinking. Excessive trauma can retard growth. I'm not certain, however, if it can cause actual shrinkage."

"What was the traumatic event that turned you blind?" said Flora.

"I'd prefer not to discuss it right now. I don't want to alarm you."

"It's not possible to alarm me," said Flora. "I'm a cynic. Nothing in human nature surprises a cynic."

"So you say," said William Spiver.

The word *cryptic* popped into Flora's head. It was preceded by the word *unnecessarily.*

"Unnecessarily cryptic," said Flora out loud.

"I beg your pardon?" said William Spiver.

But then they were at Tootie's house. They were walking through her backyard and into her kitchen, which smelled like bacon and lemons.

Tootie put Ulysses down on the table.

"I don't understand," said William Spiver. "We're back at your house, but I can still smell the squirrel."

Flora took the paper out of her pajamas. She handed it to Tootie. She felt like a spy, a successful spy, a triumphant spy. Albeit, a spy in pajamas.

"What's this?" said Tootie.

"It's proof that you aren't the victim of an extended hallucination," said Flora.

Tootie held the paper with both hands. She stared at it. "'Squirtel!'" she said.

"Squirtel?" said William Spiver.

"Keep reading," said Flora.

"'Squirtel!'" said Tootie. "'I am. Ulysses. Born anew.'"

"See?" said Flora.

"What does that prove?" said William Spiver. "What does it even mean?"

"The squirrel's name is Ulysses," said Tootie.

"Wait a minute," said William Spiver. "Are you positing that the squirrel typed those words?"

Positing? *Positing?*

"Yes," said Flora. "That's exactly what I'm positing."

"The hallucination extends," said Tootie.

"What hallucination?" said William Spiver.

"The squirrel as a superhero hallucination," said Tootie.

"Surely you jest," said William Spiver.

Ulysses sat up on his hind legs. He looked at William Spiver and then at Tootie, and finally he turned his eyes to Flora. He raised his eyebrows and gave her a look full of questions, full of hope.

Flora felt a pang of doubt. He was, after all, just a squirrel. She had no proof that he was a superhero. What if there was some other explanation for those words? Also, there was Tootie's disturbing point to consider: What kind of superhero types?

And then she thought about Alfred, how everyone doubted him, how no one (except the parakeet Dolores) knew that he was Incandesto, and how no one (except Dolores) truly believed in him.

Was it Flora's job to believe in Ulysses?

And what did that make her? A parakeet?

"Let me get this straight," said William Spiver. "You, a self-professed cynic, are positing that the squirrel is a superhero."

The words "Do not hope; instead, observe" flitted through Flora's brain.

She took a deep breath; she brushed the phrase away.

"The squirrel typed those words," she said.

"Well," said William Spiver, whose hand was still on Flora's shoulder. Why didn't he move his hand? "Let's just approach this scientifically. We'll put the squirrel in front of Great-Aunt Tootie's computer, and we'll ask him to type. Again."

CHAPTER NINETEEN
The Inadvertent *I*

He sat in front of the machine. It was different from Flora's mother's typewriter. There was a blank screen instead of paper, and the whole contraption glowed, emitting a warm but not entirely friendly smell.

The keyboard was familiar, though. Each of the letters was there, each of them in the same place.

Flora and Tootie stood behind him, and William Spiver, the boy with dark glasses, stood behind him, too.

This was an important moment. Ulysses understood that very well. Everything depended on him typing something. He had to do it for Flora.

His whiskers trembled. He could feel them trembling. He could *see* them trembling.

What could he do?

He turned and sniffed his tail.

There was nothing he could do except to be himself, to try to make the letters on the keyboard speak the truth of his heart, to work to make them reveal the essence of the squirrel he was.

But what was the truth?

And what kind of squirrel was he?

He looked around the room. There was a tall window, and

outside the window was the green, green world and the blue sky. Inside, there were shelves and shelves of books. And on the wall above the keyboard was a picture of a man and woman floating over a city. They were suspended in a golden light. The man was holding the woman, and she had one arm flung out in front of her as if she were pointing the way home. Ulysses liked the woman's face. She reminded him of Flora.

Looking at the painting made the squirrel feel warm inside, certain of something. Whoever had painted the picture loved the floating man and the floating woman. He loved the city they floated above. He loved the golden light.

Just as Ulysses loved the green world outside. And the blue sky. And Flora's round head.

His whiskers stopped trembling.

"What's happening?" asked William Spiver.

"Nothing," said Flora.

"He's gone into some kind of trance," said Tootie.

"Shhh," said Flora.

Ulysses inched closer to the keyboard.

THE SQUIRREL TYPED.

THE PEOPLE WAITED.

DESTINY BESTIRRED ITSELF. . . .

CHAPTER TWENTY
What It Said

I love your round head,
the brilliant green,
the watching blue,
these letters,
this world, you.
I am very, very hungry.

CHAPTER TWENTY-ONE
Poetry

They were sitting in Tootie's office. Tootie was on the couch with a package of frozen peas on her head. She had fainted.

Unfortunately, she had hit her head on the edge of the desk on the way down.

Fortunately, Flora had remembered an issue of ***TERRIBLE THINGS CAN HAPPEN TO YOU!*** advising that a bag of frozen peas made an excellent cold compress to "provide comfort and reduce swelling."

"Read it one more time," said William Spiver to Flora.

Flora read Ulysses's words aloud again.

"The squirrel wrote poetry," said Tootie in a voice filled with wonder.

"Keep those peas on your head," said Flora.

"I don't get the last part," said William Spiver, "the part about hunger. What does that mean?"

Flora turned away from the computer and looked at William Spiver's dark glasses and saw, again, her round-headed pajama-ed self reflected there. "It means he's hungry," she said. "He hasn't had any breakfast."

"Oh," said William Spiver. "I see. It's literal."

Ulysses was sitting on his hind legs beside the computer. He nodded hopefully.

“It’s poetry,” said Tootie from the couch.

Ulysses puffed out his chest the tiniest bit.

“Well, it might be poetry,” said William Spiver, “but it’s not great poetry. It’s not even good poetry.”

“But what does this all mean?” said Tootie.

“Why does it have to mean something?” said William Spiver. “The universe is a random place.”

“Oh, for heaven’s sake, William,” said Tootie.

Flora felt something well up inside of her. What was it? Pride in the squirrel? Annoyance at William Spiver? Wonder? Hope?

Suddenly, she remembered the words that appeared over Alfred T. Slipper’s head when he was submerged in the vat of Incandesto!

"Do you doubt him?" said Flora.

"Of course I doubt him!" said William Spiver.

"Do not," said Flora.

"Why?" said William Spiver.

She stared at him.

"Take off your glasses," she said. "I want to see your eyes."

"No," said William Spiver.

"Take them off."

"I won't."

"Children," said Tootie. "Please."

Who was William Spiver really?

Yes, yes, he was the great-nephew of Tootie Tickham suddenly (suspiciously) come to stay the summer. But who was he really? What if he was some kind of comic-book character himself? What if he was a villain whose powers were depleted as soon as the light of the world hit his eyes?

Incandesto was forever being attacked by his arch-nemesis, the Darkness of 10,000 Hands.

Every superhero had an arch-nemesis.

What if Ulysses's arch-nemesis was William Spiver?

"The truth must be known!" said Flora. She stepped forward. She reached out her hand to remove William Spiver's glasses.

And then she heard her name. "Floooooorrrrrraaaaaaa Belllllllle, your father is here!"

"Flora Belle," said William Spiver in a gentle voice.

Ulysses was still sitting on his hind legs. His ears were pricked. He looked back and forth between Flora and William Spiver.

"We have to go," said Flora.

"Wait," said William Spiver.

Flora picked Ulysses up by the scruff of his neck. She put him under her pajama top.

"Will I ever see you again?" said William Spiver.

"The universe is a random place, William Spiver," said Flora. "Who can say whether we will meet again or not?"

CHAPTER TWENTY-TWO
A Giant Ear

Her father was standing on the top step in front of the open door. He was wearing a dark suit and a tie and a hat with a brim, even though it was Saturday and summertime.

Flora's father was an accountant at the firm Flinton, Flosston, and Frick.

Flora wasn't sure, but she thought it was possible that her father was the world's loneliest man. He didn't even have Incandesto and Dolores to keep him company anymore.

"Hi, Pop," she said.

"Flora," said her father. He smiled at her, and then he sighed.

"I'm not ready yet."

"Oh, that's okay," said her father. He sighed again. "I'll wait."

He walked with Flora into the living room. He sat down on the couch. He took off his hat and balanced it on his knee.

"Are you in the house now, George?" Flora's mother shouted from the kitchen. "Is Flora with you?"

"I am inside!" shouted Flora's father. "Flora is with me!"

The *clack-clack-clack* of the typewriter echoed through the house. Silverware rattled. And then there was silence.

"What are you doing, George?" her mother shouted.

"I am sitting on the couch, Phyllis. I am waiting for my

daughter!" Flora's father moved his hat from his left knee to his right knee and then back to his left knee again.

Ulysses shifted underneath Flora's pajamas.

"What are you two going to do today?" Flora's mother shouted.

"I don't know, Phyllis!"

"I can hear you perfectly well, George," said Flora's mother as she came into the living room. "You don't need to shout. Flora, what have you got under your pajama top?"

"Nothing," said Flora.

"Is it that squirrel?"

"No," said Flora.

"What squirrel?" said Flora's father.

"Don't lie to me," said her mother.

"Okay," said Flora. "It's the squirrel. I'm keeping him."

"I knew it. I knew you were hiding something. Listen to me: that squirrel is diseased. You are engaging in dangerous behavior."

Flora turned away.

She had a superhero under her pajamas. She didn't have to listen to her mother, or anybody else for that matter. A new day was dawning, a girl-with-a-superhero kind of day. "I'm going to go change now," she said.

"This will not work, Flora Belle," said her mother. "That squirrel is not staying."

"What squirrel?" said Flora's father again.

Flora went halfway up the stairs, and then she stopped. She stood on the landing. *The Criminal Element* suggested that anyone truly invested in fighting crime, in besting criminals, should learn to listen carefully. "All words at all times, true or false, whispered or shouted, are clues to the workings of the human heart. Listen. You must, if you care to understand anything at all, become a Giant Ear."

This was what *The Criminal Element* suggested.

And this was what Flora intended to do.

She pulled Ulysses out from underneath her pajama top.

"Sit on my shoulder," she whispered to him.

Ulysses climbed up on her shoulder.

"Listen," she said.

He nodded.

Flora felt brave and capable, standing there on the landing with her squirrel on her shoulder.

"Do not hope," she whispered. "Instead, observe."

She took a deep breath and let it out slowly. She held herself absolutely still. She became a Giant Ear.

And what Flora the Giant Ear heard was astonishing.

CHAPTER TWENTY-THREE
Enter the Villain

"George," said Flora's mother, "we have a problem. Your daughter has become emotionally attached to a diseased squirrel."

"How's that?" said Flora's father.

"There's a squirrel," said her mother, speaking more slowly now, as if she were pointing at each word as she said it.

"There's a squirrel," repeated her father.

"The squirrel is not well."

"There's an unwell squirrel."

"There's a sack in the garage. And a shovel."

"Okay," said Flora's father. "There's a sack and a shovel. In the garage."

At this point, there was a very long silence.

"I need you to put the squirrel out of its misery," said Flora's mother.

"How's that?" said her father.

"For the love of Pete, George!" shouted her mother. "Put the squirrel in the sack, and then hit him over the head with the shovel."

Flora's father gasped.

Flora gasped, too. She was surprised at herself. The ladies in

her mother's romance novels put their hands on their bosoms and gasped. But Flora was not a gasper. She was a cynic.

Flora's father said, "I don't understand."

Flora's mother cleared her throat. She uttered the blood-soaked words again. She said them louder. She said them more slowly. "You put the squirrel in the sack, George. You hit the squirrel over the head with the shovel." She paused. "And then," she said, "you use the shovel to bury the squirrel."

"Put the squirrel in a sack? Hit the squirrel over the head with a shovel?" said Flora's father in a squeaky, despairing voice. "Oh, Phyllis. Oh, Phyllis, no."

"Yes," said Flora's mother. "It's the humane thing to do."

Flora understood that she had made a mistake in thinking that William Spiver was anybody important.

Everything was coming into sharp and terrifying focus; the story was starting to make sense: Ulysses was a superhero (probably), and Phyllis Buckman was his arch-nemesis (definitely).

Holy unanticipated occurrences!

CHAPTER TWENTY-FOUR
Stalked, Chased, Threatened, Poisoned, Etc.

He should have been shocked, but he wasn't, not really.

It was a sad fact of his existence as a squirrel that there was always someone, somewhere, who wanted him dead. In his short life, Ulysses had been stalked by cats, attacked by raccoons, and shot at with BB guns, slingshots, and a bow and arrow (granted, the arrow was made of rubber — but still, it had hurt). He had been shouted at, threatened, and poisoned. He had been flung ears over tail by the stream of water issuing from a garden hose turned to full force. Once, at the public picnic grounds, a small girl had tried to beat him to death with her enormous teddy bear. And last fall, a pickup truck had run over his tail.

Truthfully, the possibility of getting hit over the head with a shovel didn't seem that alarming.

Life was dangerous, particularly if you were a squirrel.

In any case, he wasn't thinking about dying. He was thinking about poetry. That is what Tootie said he had written. Poetry. He liked the word — its smallness, its density, the way it rose up at the end as if it had wings.

Poetry.

"Don't worry," said Flora. "You're a superhero. This malfeasance will be stopped!"

Ulysses dug his claws into Flora's pajamas to keep his balance on her shoulder.

"Malfeasance," said Flora again.

Poetry, thought Ulysses.

CHAPTER TWENTY-FIVE
Seal Blubber

Flora's father's car seats smelled like butterscotch and ketchup, and Flora was in the backseat, where the smell of butterscotch and ketchup was the most powerful. She had a Bootsie Boots shoe box with Ulysses in it on her lap, and she was feeling carsick even though the car wasn't moving yet. She was also feeling the tiniest bit overwhelmed.

Things, in general, were pretty confusing.

For instance, here was Ulysses, sitting in a shoe box, knowing that there was a shovel in the trunk of the car and that the man driving the car had been instructed to whack him over the head with the shovel, and the squirrel didn't look worried or afraid. He looked happy.

And then there was Flora's mother, the person who had given Flora the shoe box. ("To protect your little friend on his journey. We'll just put this washcloth in here as a comfy blanket.") She was standing at the door, smiling and waving good-bye to them as if she weren't truly a murder-planning arch-nemesis. Talk about the Darkness of 10,000 Hands.

Nothing was as it seemed.

Flora looked down at the squirrel. Of course, he was not

what he seemed, either. And that was a good thing. An Incandesto thing.

Flora felt a shiver of belief, of possibility, pass through her. Her parents had no idea what kind of squirrel they were dealing with.

Her father put the car in reverse.

As he backed out of the driveway, Flora saw William Spiver standing in Tootie's front yard. He was looking up at the sky; he turned his head slowly in the direction of the car. His glasses flashed in the sun.

Tootie appeared. She was waving one of the pink gloves as if it were a flag of surrender.

"Stop the car!" she shouted.

"Step on the gas," Flora said to her father.

She did not want to talk to Tootie. And she definitely did not want to talk to William Spiver. She didn't want to see herself reflected in his dark glasses. She had her own thoughts about the random and confusing nature of the universe. She didn't need his, too.

Also, she was in a hurry. There was a murder to stop, a superhero to mentor, villains to vanquish, darkness to eradicate. She couldn't waste time trading stupid thoughts with William Spiver.

"Flora Belle," shouted William Spiver, almost as if he were reading her mind. "I've had some interesting thoughts." He ran toward the car and fell into the bushes. "Great-Aunt Tootie," he shouted, "I need your assistance."

"What in the world is going on?" said her father. He slammed on the brakes.

"It's just a temporarily blind boy," said Flora. "And Mrs. Tickham from next door. She's his aunt. His great-aunt. Never mind. It doesn't make any difference. Keep going."

But it was too late. Tootie had helped William Spiver out of the bushes, and the two of them were walking toward the car.

William Spiver was smiling.

"Hello," her father called out to them. "I'm George Buckman. How do you do?"

Flora's father introduced himself to everyone all the time, even if the person was someone he had already met. It was an annoying and extremely persistent habit.

"Hello, sir," said William Spiver. "I am William Spiver. I would like to speak to your daughter, Flora Belle."

"I don't have time to talk to you right now, William Spiver," said Flora.

"Great-Aunt Tootie, can you assist me? Will you take me to Flora's side of the vehicle?"

"Please excuse me while I escort this extremely disturbed and neurotic child to the other side of the car," said Tootie.

"Certainly, certainly," said Flora's father. And then he said to absolutely no one, "George Buckman. How do you do?"

Flora sighed. She looked down at Ulysses. Considering the human beings she was surrounded by, believing in a squirrel seemed like an increasingly reasonable plan of action.

"I wanted to apologize," said William Spiver, who was now standing beside her window.

"For what?" said Flora.

"It wasn't the worst poetry I've ever heard."

"Oh," said Flora.

"Also, I'm sorry that I wouldn't take my glasses off when you asked me to."

"Take them off now, then," said Flora.

"I can't," said William Spiver. "They've been glued to my head by evil forces beyond my control."

"You lie," said Flora.

"Yes. No. I don't. I do. I'm engaging in hyperbole. It *seems* as if the glasses have been glued to my head." He lowered his voice. "Actually, I'm afraid that if I take my glasses off, the whole world will unravel."

"That's stupid," said Flora. "There are bigger things to worry about."

"For instance?"

Flora realized that she was going to say something to William Spiver that she hadn't intended to say; the words were out of her mouth before she could stop them.

"Do you know what an arch-nemesis is?" she whispered.

"Of course I do," William Spiver whispered back.

"Right," said Flora. "Well, Ulysses has got one. It's my mother."

William Spiver's eyebrows rose up above his dark glasses. Flora was pleased to note that he looked properly surprised and shocked.

"Speaking of Ulysses," said Tootie, "I have some poetry that I would like to recite to him."

"Are you sure that now is the time for a poetry recitation?" said William Spiver.

Ulysses sat up straighter in his Bootsie Boots shoe box. He looked at Tootie. He nodded.

"I was moved by your poetry," said Tootie to the squirrel.

Ulysses puffed out his chest.

"And I have some poetry that I would like to recite to you in honor of the recent, um, transformations in your life." Tootie put a hand on her chest. "This is Rilke," she said. "'You, sent out beyond your recall, / go to the limits of your longing. / Embody me. / Flare up like flame / and make big shadows I can move in.'"

Ulysses stared up at Tootie, his eyes bright.

"'Flare up like flame'!" said Flora's father from the front seat. "That is moving, yes. That is quite lovely, flaring up like flame. Thank you so much. We have to be on our way now."

"But will you return?" said William Spiver.

Angelou
Joyce
Keats
Shelley
Wilde
The
World's
Vol
II
FU1PGWT3
SIZE 3
GLORIA WEDGE
CHERRY
Bootsie
Boots

Flora looked up and saw William Spiver's words hanging in the air above him like a small, tattered flag.

But will you return?

"I'm just spending the afternoon with my father, William Spiver," she said. "It's not like I'm heading off to the South Pole."

TERRIBLE THINGS CAN HAPPEN TO YOU! had done an extensive piece on what to do if you were stranded at the South Pole. Their advice could be summed up in three simple words: "Eat seal blubber."

It was astonishing, really, what people could live through. Flora felt cheered up all of a sudden, just thinking about eating seal blubber and doing impossible things, surviving when the odds were against her and her squirrel.

They would figure out a way to outwit the arch-nemesis! They would triumph over the shovel and the sack! And they would triumph together, like Dolores and Incandesto!

"I'm glad," said William Spiver. "I'm glad that you're not going to the South Pole, Flora Belle."

Flora's father cleared his throat. "George Buckman," he said. "How do you do?"

"It was nice to meet you, sir," said William Spiver.

"Remember those words," said Tootie.

"'Flare up like flame,'" said Flora's father.

"I was speaking to the squirrel," said Tootie.

"Of course," said Flora's father. "My apologies. The squirrel."

"I will see you again," said William Spiver.

"Beware the arch-nemesis," said Flora.

"I will see you again," said William Spiver.

"We're off to fight evil," said Flora as her father backed the car out of the driveway.

William Spiver waved at the car. "I will see you again!"

He seemed so stuck on the idea of seeing her again that Flora didn't have the heart to tell him that he was waving in the wrong direction.

CHAPTER TWENTY-SIX
Spies Don't Cry

Flora's father was a careful driver. He kept his left hand at ten o'clock on the steering wheel and his right hand at two. He never took his eyes off the road. He did not go fast.

"Speed," her father often said. "That is what will kill you, that and taking your eyes off the road. Never, ever take your eyes off the road."

"Pop," said Flora, "I need to talk to you."

"Okay," said her father. He kept his eyes on the road. "About what?"

"That sack. And that shovel."

"What sack?" said her father. "What shovel?"

It occurred to Flora that her father would make an excellent spy. He never really answered questions. Instead, when asked a question, he simply responded with a nifty sidestep or a question of his own.

For instance, when her parents were getting their divorce, Flora had a conversation with her father that went something like this:

FLORA: Are you and Mom getting divorced?

FLORA'S FATHER: Who says we're getting divorced?

FLORA: Mom.

FLORA'S FATHER: Is that what she said?

FLORA: That's what she said.

FLORA'S FATHER: I wonder why she said that.

And then he started to cry.

Spies probably didn't cry. But still.

"There's a sack and a shovel in the trunk of the car, Pop," said Flora.

"Is there?" said her father.

"I saw you put them in there."

"It's true. I did put a sack and a shovel in the trunk of the car."

The Criminal Element said that it was a good idea to engage in relentless, open-ended questioning. "If you question with enough ferocity, people are sometimes surprised into answering questions that they do not intend to answer. When in doubt, question. Question more. Question faster."

"Why?" said Flora.

"I intend to dig a hole," said her father.

"For what?" said Flora.

"A thing that I am going to bury."

"What thing are you going to bury?"

"A sack!"

"Why are you burying a sack?"

"Because your mother asked me to."

"Why did she ask you to bury a sack?"

Her father tapped his fingers on the steering wheel. He stared straight ahead. "Why did she ask me to bury a sack?

Why did she ask me to bury a sack? That's a good one. Hey, I know! Do you want to get something to eat?"

"What?" said Flora.

"How about some lunch?" said her father.

"For the love of Pete!" said Flora.

"Or some breakfast? How about we stop and eat a meal, any meal?"

Flora sighed.

The Criminal Element advised "stalling, delaying, and obfuscation of every possible sort" when it came to dealing with a criminal.

Her father wasn't a criminal. Not exactly. But he *had* been enlisted in the service of villainy—basically, he was in cahoots with an arch-nemesis. So maybe it would be good to stall, to delay the inevitable showdown, by going into a restaurant.

Besides, the squirrel was hungry, and he would need to be strong for the battle ahead.

"Okay," said Flora. "Okay. Sure. Let's eat."

CHAPTER TWENTY-SEVEN
The World in All Its Smelly Glory

Okay. Sure. Let's eat.

What wonderful words those are, thought Ulysses.

Let's eat.

Talk about poetry.

The squirrel was happy.

He was happy because he was with Flora.

He was happy because he had the words from Tootie's poem flowing through his head and heart.

He was happy because he was going to be fed soon.

And he was happy because he was, well, *happy.*

He climbed out of the shoe box and put his front paws on the door and his nose out the open window.

He was a squirrel riding in a car on a summer day with someone he loved. His whiskers and nose were in the breeze.

And there were so many smells!

Overflowing trash cans, just-cut grass, sun-warmed patches of pavement, the loamy richness of dirt, earthworms (loamy-smelling, too; often difficult to distinguish from the smell of dirt), dog, more dog, dog again (Oh, dogs! Small dogs, large dogs, foolish dogs; the torturing of dogs was the one reliable pleasure of a squirrel's existence), the tang of fertilizer, a faint whiff of birdseed, something baking, the hidden hint of nuttiness (pecan, acorn), the small, apologetic, don't-mind-me odor of mouse, and the ruthless stench of cat. (Cats were terrible; cats were never to be trusted. Never.)

The world in all its smelly glory, in all its treachery and joy and nuttiness, washed over Ulysses, ran through him, filled him. He could smell everything. He could even smell the blue of the sky.

He wanted to capture it. He wanted to write it down. He wanted to tell Flora. He turned and looked at her.

"Keep your eyes open for malfeasance," she said to him.

Ulysses nodded.

The words from Tootie's poem sounded in his head. "'Flare up like flame'!"

Yes, he thought. *That's what I'll do. I'll flare up like flame, and I'll write it all down.*

CHAPTER TWENTY-EIGHT
The Giant Do-Nut

"You'll have to leave the squirrel in the car," said Flora's father as he pulled into the parking lot of the Giant Do-Nut.

"No," said Flora. "It's too hot."

"I'll leave the windows down," said her father.

"Someone will steal him."

"You think someone would steal him?" Her father sounded doubtful, but hopeful. "Who would steal a squirrel?"

"A criminal," said Flora.

The Criminal Element spoke often, and passionately, about the nefarious activities that every human being is capable of. Not only did it insist that the human heart was dark beyond all reckoning; it also likened the heart to a river. And further, it said, "If we are not careful, that river can carry us along in its hidden currents of want and anger and need, and transform each of us into the very criminal we fear."

"The human heart is a deep, dark river with hidden currents," Flora said to her father. "Criminals are everywhere."

Her father tapped his fingers on the steering wheel. "I wish I could disagree with you, but I can't."

Ulysses sneezed.

"Bless you," said her father.

"I'm not leaving him," said Flora.

Alfred T. Slipper took his parakeet, Dolores, with him everywhere, sometimes even to the offices of the Paxatawket Life Insurance Company. "Not without my parakeet." That was what Alfred said.

"Not without my squirrel," said Flora.

If her father recognized the sentence, if the words reminded him of their time together reading about Incandesto, he didn't show it. He merely sighed. "Bring him in, then," he said. "But keep the lid on the shoe box."

Ulysses climbed into the shoe box, and Flora dutifully lowered the lid on his small face.

"Okay," she said. "All right."

She climbed out of the car, and then she stood and looked up at the Giant Do-Nut sign.

GIANT DO-NUTS INSIDE! the sign screamed in neon letters, while an extremely large donut disappeared over and over again into a cup of coffee.

But there was no hand on the donut. *Who,* Flora wondered, *is doing the dunking?* A small shiver ran down her spine.

What if we are all donuts just waiting to be dunked? she thought.

It was the kind of question that William Spiver would ask. She could hear him asking it. It was also the kind of question that William Spiver would have an answer for. That was the thing about William Spiver. He always had an answer, even if it was an annoying one.

"Listen to me," she whispered to the shoe box. "You are not a donut waiting to be dunked. You are a superhero. Do not let yourself be tricked or fooled. Remember the shovel. Keep an eye on George Buckman."

Her father got out of the car. He put his hands in his pockets and jingled his change. "Shall we?" he said.

Stall! Delay! Obfuscate!

"Let's," said Flora.

CHAPTER TWENTY-NINE
Cootchie-Coo

The Giant Do-Nut smelled like fried eggs and donuts and other people's closets. The dining room was full of laughter and donut dunking.

A waitress sat Flora and her father at a booth in the corner and handed them glossy, enormous menus. Flora surreptitiously (*The Criminal Element* recommended surreptitious action at all possible junctures) removed the lid from the shoe box. Ulysses poked his head out and looked around the restaurant. And then he turned his attention to the menu. He stared at it with a dreamy look on his face.

"Get whatever you want," said Flora's father. "Order your heart's desire."

Ulysses emitted a happy sigh.

"Pay attention," whispered Flora.

A waitress came and stood over them. She tapped her pencil on the order pad.

"What can I get you?" she said.

Her name tag spelled out her name in all-capital letters: RITA!

Flora narrowed her eyes. The exclamation point made Rita seem untrustworthy, or, at the very least, insincere.

"Well," said Rita. "What's it gonna be?" Her hair was piled up very, very high on her head. She looked like Marie Antoinette.

Not that Flora had ever seen Marie Antoinette, but she had read about her in a ***TERRIBLE THINGS CAN HAPPEN TO YOU!*** issue on the French Revolution. Marie Antoinette, from the little bit that Flora knew about her, would have made a very bad waitress.

Flora suddenly remembered that she had a squirrel in her lap. She tapped Ulysses on the head again. "Lie low," she whispered to him, "but be prepared." She arranged the washcloth so that he was almost completely hidden.

"Whatcha got there?" asked Rita.

"Where?" said Flora.

"In the box," said Rita. "Got a baby doll in the box? Are you talking to your baby doll?"

"Talking to my baby doll?" said Flora. She felt a flush of outrage crawl up her cheeks. For the love of Pete! She was ten years old, almost eleven. She knew how to administer CPR. She knew how to outwit an arch-nemesis. She was acquainted with the profound importance of seal blubber. She was the sidekick to a superhero.

Plus she was a cynic.

What self-respecting cynic would carry around a doll in a shoe box?

"I do not," said Flora. "Have. A. Baby. Doll."

"Let me see her," said Rita. "Don't be shy." She bent over. Her big Marie Antoinette hair scraped against Flora's chin.

"No," said Flora.

"George Buckman," said Flora's father in a worried voice. "How do you do?"

"Cootchie-coo," said Rita.

Flora felt a very pointed, very specific sense of doom.

Rita poked her pencil into the shoe box slowly, slowly. She pushed the washcloth around. Slowly. And the washcloth (oh, so slowly) fell back and revealed Ulysses's whiskered face.

"George Buckman," said her father in a much louder voice. "How do you do?"

Rita screamed a long and impossibly loud scream.

Ulysses screamed in return.

And then he leaped from the shoe box.

At this point, things stopped proceeding at such a leisurely pace.

The squirrel was airborne, and time swung back into action with a vengeance.

At last! thought Flora. *It's Incandesto time!*

CHAPTER THIRTY
Sunny-Side Up!

He had never been so frightened in his life. Never. The woman's face was monstrous. Her hair was monstrous. And the word on her name tag (RITA!) appeared monstrous to him, too.

Be calm, he told himself as she poked her pencil around. He held himself as still as he could.

But then Rita screamed.

And it was absolutely impossible not to answer her long, piercing shriek with a piercing shriek of his own.

She screamed; he screamed.

And then every one of his animal instincts kicked in. He acted without thinking. He tried to escape. He leaped from the box and ended up, somehow, exactly where he did not want to be: in the middle of the monstrous hair.

Rita jumped up and down. She put her hands to her head. She swatted and clawed, trying to dislodge him. The harder she hit him, the higher she jumped, the more fiercely the squirrel clung.

In this way, Rita and Ulysses danced together around the Giant Do-Nut.

"What's happening?" someone shouted.

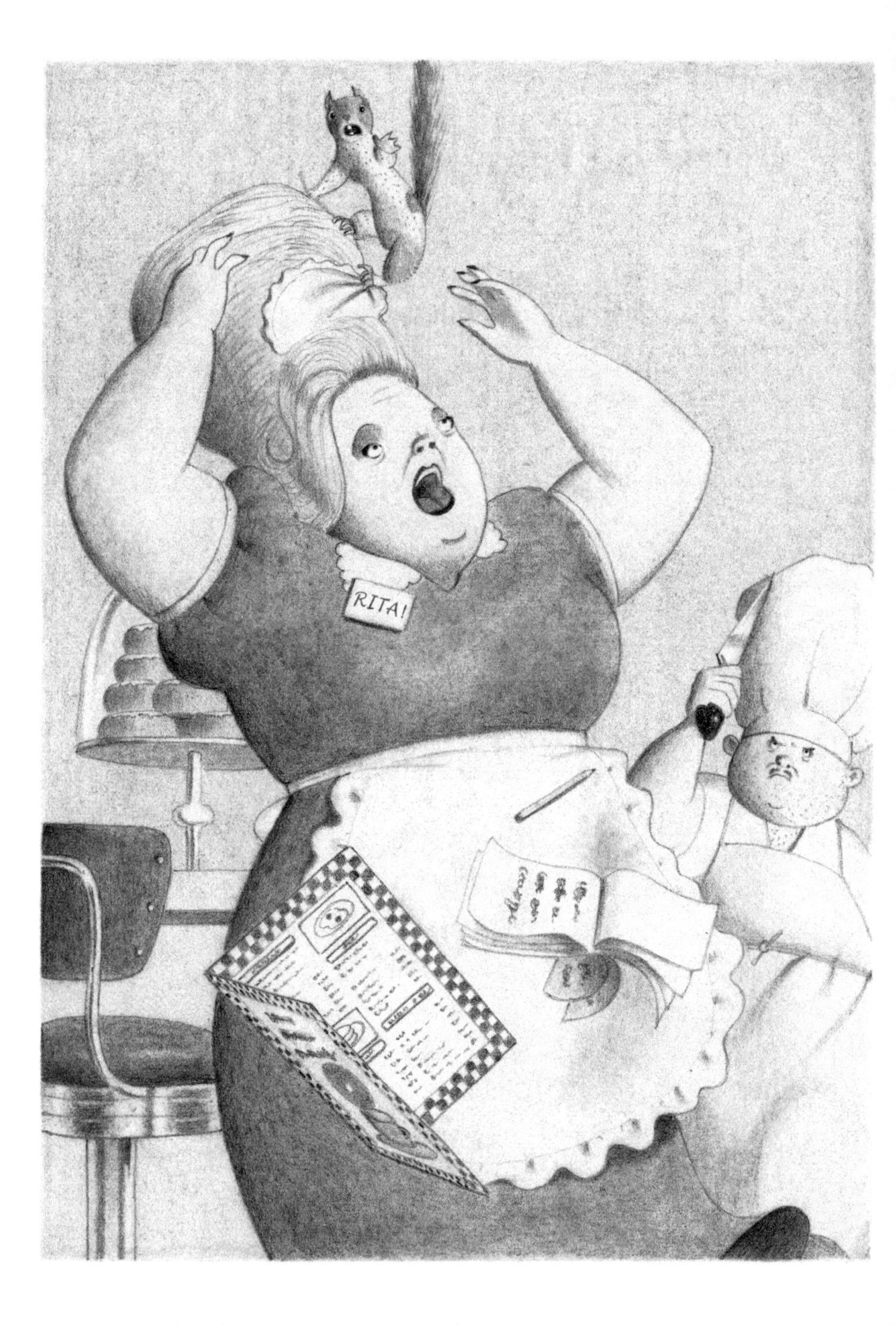
RITA!

"Her hair is on fire," someone answered.

"No, no, there's something in her hair," another person shouted. "And it's alive!"

"Arrrrgggghhhhhh!" screamed Rita. "Helppp meeeeeee!"

How, Ulysses wondered, had things gone so wrong?

Only moments ago, he had been looking at the Giant Do-Nut menu, captivated by the glossy pictures of food and the dazzling descriptions that accompanied the pictures.

There were giant donuts with sprinkles, giant donuts powdered, iced! Giant donuts filled with things: jelly, cream, chocolate.

He had never had a giant donut.

Actually, he had never had any kind of donut.

They looked delicious. All of them. How was a squirrel to choose?

And to complicate matters, there were eggs: scrambled, poached, over easy, sunny-side up.

Sunny-side up! thought Ulysses as he clung to Rita's hair. *What a wonderful phrase!*

A man emerged from the kitchen. He had on a gigantic white hat, and he was holding something metal that flashed in the overhead lights of the Giant Do-Nut. It was a knife.

"Help me!" screamed Rita.

And me, thought Ulysses. *Help me, too.*

But he was quite certain that the man with the knife had no intention of helping him.

And then he heard Flora's voice. He couldn't see her because Rita was now spinning around, and everything in the restaurant had become somewhat blurred—all the faces had become one face; all the screams had become one scream.

But Flora's voice stood out. It was the voice of the person he loved. He concentrated on her words. He worked to understand her.

"Ulysses!" she shouted. "Ulysses! Remember who you are!"

Remember who he was?

Who was he?

As if Flora had heard his unspoken question, she answered him, "You're Ulysses!"

That's right, he thought. *I am.*

"Act!" shouted Flora.

This was good advice. Flora was absolutely right. He was Ulysses, and he must act.

The man with the knife stepped toward Rita.

Ulysses loosened his hold on her hair. He leaped again. This time he leaped with purpose and intent. He leaped with all his strength.

He flew.

CHAPTER THIRTY-ONE
Holy Unanticipated Occurrences

Flora watched Ulysses fly over her, his tail extended at full length and his front paws delicately pointed. It was just like her dream. He looked incredibly, undeniably heroic.

"Holy bagumba," said Flora.

She climbed on top of the booth so that she had a better view.

When Incandesto flew, when he became a brilliant streak of light in the darkness of the world, he was usually headed somewhere, to save someone, and Dolores was always flying at his side, offering advice, encouragement, and wisdom.

Flora wasn't sure exactly what Ulysses was doing, and it didn't look like he really knew, either. But he was flying.

"George Buckman," whispered her father. "How do you do?"

Flora had forgotten about her father. He was looking up at Ulysses. And he was smiling. It wasn't a sad smile. It was a happy smile.

"Pop?" said Flora.

There was a long, loud scream from Rita. "It was in my hair!" she shouted.

Someone threw a donut at Ulysses.

A baby started to cry.

Flora climbed out of the booth so that she could stand next to her father. She slipped her hand into his.

"Holy unanticipated occurrences," said Flora's father in the voice of Dolores.

It had been a long time since Flora had heard her father say those words.

"His name is Ulysses," she told him.

Her father looked at her. He raised his eyebrows. "Ulysses," he said. He shook his head. And then he laughed. It was a single syllable. "Ha."

And then he laughed longer. "Ha-ha-ha."

Flora's heart opened up inside of her. "Do not hope," she whispered to it.

And then she noticed that the cook was leaping and twirling, waving his knife and trying to reach the flying squirrel.

She looked up at her father. She said, "This malfeasance must be stopped. Right?"

"Right," said her father.

And since her father agreed with her, Flora stuck out her foot and tripped the man with the knife.

CHAPTER THIRTY-TWO
Sprinkles

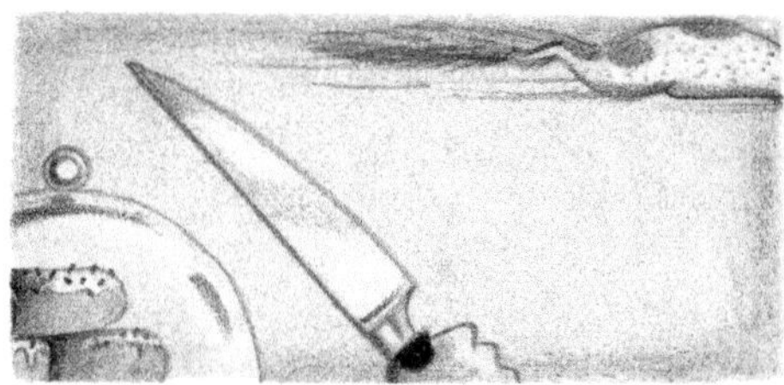

I FLEW!

WHERE'S FLORA?

IS THAT A PIECE
OF DONUT?

SPRINKLES!

CHAPTER THIRTY-THREE
Does Rabies Itch?

His eyes were closed. His head was bleeding. Flora knew from *TERRIBLE THINGS CAN HAPPEN TO YOU!* that head wounds bleed excessively, whether they are bad or not.

"All head wounds bleed excessively," she said to her father. "Don't panic."

"Okay," said her father. "Use this." He handed her his tie.

Flora knelt down. She had a very powerful sense of déjà vu. Was it just yesterday that she had bent over the body of an unknown squirrel in Tootie's backyard?

"Ulysses?" she said. She dabbed at the blood with the tie.

The squirrel didn't open his eyes.

An eerie quiet descended. The whole of the Giant Do-Nut became preternaturally calm. Everything—the donuts, the squirrel, her father—seemed to hold its breath.

Flora knew what was happening. She had read about it in *TERRIBLE THINGS CAN HAPPEN TO YOU!* It was the calm before the storm: The air becomes still. The birds stop singing. The world waits.

And then the storm comes.

Inside the Giant Do-Nut, there was a moment of deep quiet, of collectively held breath. And then someone said, "I think it was a rat."

"But it was flying," said another voice.

"It was in my hair," said Rita.

The cook shouted, "I'm gonna call the cops! That's what I'm gonna do!"

Rita was right behind him. "Forget about the cops, Ernie. Call the ambulance. I have rabies. It was in my hair."

"You," said Ernie. He pointed at Flora with his knife. "You tripped me."

"That's her," said Rita. "She's the one. Plus she brought that thing in here in the first place. Dressed it up like a baby doll."

"I did not," said Flora, "dress him up like a baby doll. And this is all your fault."

The Criminal Element said that sometimes it was wise to put criminals on the defensive by making "slanderous or blatantly untrue comments. The surprising unfairness of this tactic will often stop criminals in their tracks."

It seemed to work.

Rita blinked. She opened her mouth and closed it again. "*My* fault?" she said.

Flora bent over Ulysses and put a finger on his chest. She felt his heart beating in a slow, thoughtful way. Gratitude and relief washed through her. And her own heart, which had been beating much too quickly, slowed inside her chest. It answered the squirrel's heart with its own measured *thud, thud, thud.*

Ulysses, her heart seemed to say. *Ulysses.*

"I'm calling the cops," said Ernie.

"George Buckman. How do you do!" shouted Flora's father. "Is there any reason to call the police?"

"Well, for one," said Rita, "it was in my hair."

"Do you think that the police should be notified of a squirrel in your hair?" said Flora's father.

The idiocy of this question, its unsettling logic, made Flora suddenly grateful for her father. She picked up Ulysses and cradled him in her left arm.

"I think I can feel the rabies coming on," said Rita. "My stomach itches."

"Does rabies itch?" said Flora's father.

"I'm gonna call somebody," said Ernie. "She tripped me."

"Whom do you think it would be wise to call in this matter of the tripping?" said Flora's father. He opened the door. He gestured for Flora to walk through it. She did.

The door swung shut behind them.

"Run!" said her father.

And they both began to run.

At some point, Flora's father started to laugh again. It wasn't a "ha-ha-ha" kind of laugh. It was a "whooooo-wheeeee" kind of laugh.

Hysteria, thought Flora.

She knew what to do for hysteria. Her father needed to be slapped. Unfortunately, there wasn't time right now. They had to make their getaway.

Her father laughed all the way to the car. He laughed when

they were in the car. He laughed as he placed his hands at ten o'clock and two. He laughed as he backed out of the parking lot and drove away from the Giant Do-Nut.

He stopped laughing only once, long enough for him to shout, "Holy bagumba!" in the voice of Dolores the parakeet.

And then he went back to laughing.

CHAPTER THIRTY-FOUR
The Getaway

They were making their getaway, but they were making their getaway slowly. Because even when Flora's father was thinking that things were hilarious, even when he was talking like a parakeet, he still, apparently, did not believe in speeding.

Flora kept looking behind them to see if they were being followed by the cops. Or Rita and Ernie.

When she finally looked down at Ulysses, his eyes were still closed, and a terrible thought occurred to her.

"What if he has a concussion?" she said to her father.

Her father, of course, laughed.

Flora tried to remember what ***TERRIBLE THINGS CAN HAPPEN TO YOU!*** said about concussions. There was something about making the person with the head injury speak a favorite nursery rhyme so that speech patterns — slurring, et cetera — could be evaluated.

Flora stared at the squirrel.

He couldn't speak. Also, she doubted he knew any nursery rhymes.

There was a very small cut on his head, but the bleeding had stopped and he was breathing softly, regularly.

"Ulysses?" she said.

And then she remembered, in its entirety, an ominous sentence from **TERRIBLE THINGS!** "It is absolutely imperative that you keep the potentially concussed patient awake at all times."

She shook the squirrel gently. His eyes stayed closed. She shook him harder and he opened his eyes and then closed them again.

Flora's heart thudded once and then dropped all the way down to her toes. She was suddenly terrified.

"Do superheroes die?" she said out loud.

Her father stopped laughing. "Listen," he said. "We won't let him die."

Flora's heart thudded again, a different kind of thud. It wasn't fear this time. It was hope.

"Does that mean that you won't try to hit him over the head with a shovel?" she said.

"I won't," said her father.

"Ever?"

"Ever."

"You promise?"

"I promise."

Her father looked at her in the rearview mirror. Flora looked back.

"Let's go to your place, then," she said. "He'll be safe there."

At these words, George Buckman started laughing hysterically. Again.

CHAPTER THIRTY-FIVE
Fear Smells

Flora's father never walked through the hallways of the Blixen Arms.

He ran.

And Flora Buckman, holding her possibly concussed squirrel, ran with him.

Flora and George Buckman ran because the Blixen Arms was owned and managed by a man named Mr. Klaus, who was in possession of an enormous, angry orange cat also named Mr. Klaus. The cat Mr. Klaus prowled the hallways of the Blixen Arms, peeing on the residents' doors and vomiting in the stairwells.

Mr. Klaus was also notorious for hiding in the green gloom of the hallways and waiting until some unlucky person stepped out of the door of his or her apartment (or into the main entrance of the Blixen Arms or down into the basement laundry room) and then pouncing on the person's ankles, biting and scratching and growling — and sometimes (weirdly enough) purring.

Flora's father's ankles were deeply scarred.

"The cat can smell your fear!" Flora shouted as she ran. "It's a scientific fact."

She had read about fear in **TERRIBLE THINGS CAN HAPPEN TO YOU!** "Fear smells," said **TERRIBLE THINGS!** "And the smell of fear further incites the predator."

Ahead of her, her father laughed his hearty and seemingly endless laugh.

If Flora had more time, she would have said, "For the love of Pete, what's so funny?"

But she didn't have time.

There was a squirrel to save.

CHAPTER THIRTY-SIX
Surprise. Anger. Joy.

Flora stood and stared at the sign on apartment 267. It was made of fake wood and engraved with white letters that spelled out the words RESIDING WITHIN: THE DR.'S MEESCHAM!

What was the apostrophe doing there? Did the doctor own the Meescham? And what was it with exclamation marks? Did people not know what they were for?

Surprise, anger, joy—that's what exclamation marks were for. They had nothing to do with who resided where.

But at this particular moment, the exclamation mark seemed entirely appropriate. It *was* terribly exciting that a doctor (who didn't know how to use apostrophes) lived in apartment 267.

"What are you staring at?" said her father. He was putting his key into the door of apartment 271, and he was laughing softly.

"A doctor lives here," said Flora.

"Dr. Meescham," said her father.

"I'm going to see if he can help with Ulysses," said Flora.

"Excellent idea," said her father. He opened the door of his apartment. He looked to the left and then to the right. "Keep your eyes open for Mr. Klaus!" he said. "I'll join you in a bit!"

He slammed the door just as Flora raised her hand to knock on Dr. Meescham's door.

267
Residing
within:
The Dr.'s
eescham!

But she didn't get the chance to knock.

The door swung open of its own accord. An old lady stood there smiling, her dentures glowing white in the perpetual green twilight of the hallway. Someone inside the apartment was screaming. No, someone was singing. It was opera. Opera music.

"At last," said the old lady. "I'm so glad to see your face."

Flora turned and looked behind her.

"I am speaking to you, little flower."

"Me?" said Flora.

"Yes, you. Little flower. Flora Belle. Beloved of your father, Mr. George Buckman. Come in, little flower. Come in."

"Actually," said Flora, "I'm looking for a doctor. I have a medical emergency."

"Of course, of course," said the old woman. "We are, all of us, medical emergencies! You must come in now. I have been waiting for so long."

She reached out and yanked Flora over the threshold of 267 and into the apartment.

The Criminal Element had a lot to say about entering the home of a stranger. They suggested that you do so at your own risk, and that if you did make the (questionable) decision to enter the home of someone you didn't know, a door to the outside world should be left open at all times to facilitate a quick escape.

The old lady slammed the door shut.

The opera music was very loud now.

Flora looked down at the hand that was on her arm. It was spotted and wrinkled.

Beloved? thought Flora. *Me?*

CHAPTER THIRTY-SEVEN
Singing with the Angels

He woke with a single, giant watery eye staring at him.

He blinked. His head hurt. The gigantic eye was mesmerizing and beautiful. It was like staring at a small planet, a whole sad and lonely world.

Ulysses found it hard to look away.

He stared at the eye, and the eye stared back.

Was he dead? Had he been hit over the head with a shovel?

He could hear someone singing. He knew he should be afraid, but he didn't feel afraid. So much had happened to him in the last twenty-four hours that somewhere along the way, he had stopped worrying. Everything had become interesting, as opposed to worrisome.

If he was dead, well, that was interesting, too.

"My eyesight is not what it was," said a voice. "When I was a girl in Blundermeecen, I could read the sign before anyone else even saw the sign. Not that it helped me, seeing things clearly. Sometimes, it is safer not to see. In Blundermeecen, the words on the sign were often not the truth. And I ask you: What good does it do you to read the words of a lie? But that is a different story. I will tell that story later. I find this magnifying glass to be of great assistance. Yes. Yes. I see him. He is very much alive."

"I know he's alive," said another voice. "I can tell that."

Flora! Flora was here with him. How comforting.

"Hmmm, yes. I see. He is a squirrel."

"For the love of Pete!" said Flora. "I know he's a squirrel."

"He is missing much fur," said the voice.

"What kind of doctor are you?" said Flora.

The voices in the room kept singing. They were full of sadness and love and desperation. The voice belonging to the giant eye hummed along with them.

Ulysses tried to get to his feet.

A gentle hand pushed him back.

"I am the Dr. Meescham who is the doctor of philosophy," said the voice. "My husband, the other Dr. Meescham, was the medical doctor. But he has passed away. This is a euphemism, of course. I mean to say that he is dead. He is departed from this world. He is elsewhere and singing with the angels. Ha, there is another euphemism: singing with the angels. I ask you, why is it so hard to stay away from the euphemisms? They creep in, always, and attempt to make the difficult things more pleasing. So. Let me try again. He is dead, the other Dr. Meescham, the medical one. And I hope that he is somewhere singing. Perhaps singing something from Mozart. But who knows where he is and what he is doing?"

"For the love of Pete!" said Flora again. "I need a medical doctor. Ulysses might have a concussion."

"Shhh, shhh, calm, calm. Why are you so agitated? There

is no need to worry. You are worried about what? You will tell me what happened that makes you think concussion."

"He hit a door," said Flora. "With his head."

"Hmmm, yes. This could give a concussion. When I was a girl in Blundermeecen, people were often getting concussions—gifts from the trolls, you understand."

"Gifts from the trolls?" said Flora. "What are you talking about? Look at him. Does he look like he has a concussion?"

The gigantic eye of Dr. Meescham came closer, much closer. It studied him. The beautiful voices sang. Dr. Meescham hummed. Ulysses felt strangely peaceful. If he spent the rest of his life being stared at by a giant eye and hummed over, things could be worse.

"The pupils of his little eyes are not dilated," said Dr. Meescham.

"Dilated pupils," said Flora. "I couldn't remember that one."

"So, this is good. This is a hopeful sign. Next we will see if he remembers what happened. We will check for amnesia."

Flora's face came into view. He was glad to see her and her round head. "Ulysses," she said, "do you remember what happened? Do you remember being in the Giant Do-Nut?"

Did he remember being in Rita's hair? Did he remember Rita screaming? Did he remember the man with the knife? Did he remember flying? Did he remember hitting his head very hard? Did he remember *not* getting to eat a giant donut? Let's see: Yes, yes, yes, yes, yes. And yes.

He nodded.

"Oh," said Dr. Meescham. "He nods his head. He communicates with you."

"He's, um, different. Special," said Flora. "A special kind of squirrel."

"Excellent! Good! I believe this!"

"Something happened to him."

"Yes, he hit a door with his head."

"No," said Flora, "before that. He was vacuumed. You know, sucked up in a vacuum cleaner."

There was a small silence. And then there was more humming from Dr. Meescham. Ulysses tried again to get to his feet and was again pushed gently back.

"You are speaking euphemistically?" said Dr. Meescham.

"I'm not," said Flora. "I'm speaking literally. He was vacuumed. It changed him."

"Certainly it did!" said Dr. Meescham. "Absolutely, it changed him to be vacuumed." She raised her magnifying glass to her eye and leaned in close, studying him. She lowered the magnifying glass. "How did it change him, please?"

Ulysses stood on all fours, and no one pushed him back.

"You will speak without euphemisms," said Dr. Meescham.

"He has powers," said Flora. "He's strong. And he can fly." She paused. "Also, he types. He writes, um, poetry."

"A typewriter! Poetry! Flight!" said Dr. Meescham. She sounded delighted.

"His name is Ulysses."

"This," said Dr. Meescham, "is an important name."

"Well," said Flora, "it was the name of the vacuum cleaner that almost killed him."

Dr. Meescham looked Ulysses in the eye.

It was rare for someone to look a squirrel in the eye.

Ulysses pulled himself up straighter. He looked back at Dr. Meescham. He met her gaze.

"You must also list among his powers the ability to understand. This is no small thing, to understand," Dr. Meescham said to Flora. And then she turned back to Ulysses. "You are feeling maybe a little sick to the stomach?"

Ulysses shook his head.

"Good," said Dr. Meescham. She clapped her hands together. "I am thinking that Ulysses is not concussed. There is only this little cut on his head, other than that: fine, good, great! I am thinking that maybe the squirrel is hungry."

Ulysses nodded.

Yes, yes! He was very hungry. He would like eggs sunny-side up.

He would like a donut. With sprinkles.

CHAPTER THIRTY-EIGHT
Unremitting Darkness

"You," said Dr. Meescham to Flora, "will have a seat on the sofa and listen to the Mozart, and I will go and make us some sandwiches."

"What about my father?" said Flora. "Shouldn't I tell him where I am?"

"Mr. George Buckman knows where you are," said Dr. Meescham. "He knows that you are safe. So, good. All is good. You will sit on the horsehair sofa, please."

Dr. Meescham went into the kitchen, and Flora turned and looked at the couch. It was a huge couch. She dutifully sat down on it and then slowly, very slowly, slid off it.

"Wow," she said.

She climbed back up on the couch and concentrated on staying put. She sat with her hands on either side of her and her legs straight out in front of her. She felt like an oversize doll. She also felt very, very tired. And a tiny bit confused.

Maybe I'm in shock, she thought.

TERRIBLE THINGS CAN HAPPEN TO YOU! had done an issue listing the symptoms of shock, but Flora couldn't remember what they were.

Was one of the symptoms of shock that you couldn't remember the symptoms of shock?

She looked over at Ulysses. He was still sitting on the dining-room table. He looked confused, too.

She waved at him, and he nodded back.

And then she noticed that there was a picture hanging on the wall opposite the couch. It was a painting of what looked like nothing but darkness. Unremitting darkness.

"Unremitting darkness" was a phrase that occurred often in ***The Criminal Element,*** but why would someone paint a picture of unremitting darkness?

Flora slid off the couch and walked over to the painting and stared at it more closely. In the middle of all the darkness, there was a tiny boat. It was floating on a black sea. Flora put her face right up against the painting. Something was wrapped around the boat, some tentacled shadow.

For the love of Pete! The tiny boat on the dark sea was getting eaten by a giant squid.

Flora's heart protested with a small thud of fear. "Holy bagumba," she whispered.

From the kitchen, there came the sound of clinking silverware and crashing plates. The opera music ended.

"Ulysses?" said Flora.

She looked behind her and saw the squirrel sitting on the floor, sniffing his tail.

"Come here," she said to him.

He walked over to her, and she picked him up and put him on her shoulder. "Look," she said.

He stared at the painting.

"This boat is getting eaten by a gigantic squid."

He nodded.

"It's a tragedy," said Flora. "There are people on board that boat. Look, you can see them. They're ant-size. But they're people."

Ulysses squinted. He nodded again.

"They're all going to die," explained Flora. "Every last one of them. As a superhero, you should be outraged. You should want to save them. Incandesto would!"

"Ah," said Dr. Meescham, coming up behind them, "you are studying my poor, lonely giant squid."

"Lonely?" said Flora.

"The giant squid is the loneliest of all God's creatures. He can sometimes go for the whole of his life without seeing another of his kind."

For some reason, Dr. Meescham's words conjured up the face of William Spiver, white haired and dark eyed. Flora's heart squinched up. *Go away, William Spiver,* she thought.

"That squid is a villain," said Flora out loud. "He needs to be vanquished. He's eating a boat. And he's going to eat all the people on the boat."

"Yes, well, loneliness makes us do terrible things," said Dr. Meescham. "And that is why the picture is there, to remind me of this. Also, because the other Dr. Meescham painted it when he was young and joyful."

HANS CHRISTIAN ANDERSEN
Sonnets to Orpheus
R.M. Rilke
Sonnets
The Hobbit
J.R.R. Tolkien
by J.R.R. Tolkien
The Tempest
Shakespeare
HAWKING

Good grief, thought Flora. *What did he paint when he was old and depressed?*

"Now, you will sit on the horsehair sofa, please," said Dr. Meescham, "and I will bring out the jelly sandwiches."

Flora sat down on the couch. Ulysses was still on her shoulder. She put up her hand and touched him. He was warm. He was a small engine of warmness.

"The giant squid is the loneliest creature in all existence," said Flora out loud.

And then, to keep things grounded and in perspective, she muttered, "Seal blubber."

And then she whispered, "Do not hope; instead, observe."

She kept her hand on the squirrel.

CHAPTER THIRTY-NINE
The Tears Roll Off

Dr. Meescham came out of the kitchen holding a pink plate with small sandwiches on it. She sat down next to Flora.

"You are enjoying the horsehair sofa," she said to Flora.

"I guess," said Flora. She wasn't sure exactly how someone enjoyed a horsehair sofa.

"You will eat a jelly sandwich," said Dr. Meescham. She extended the plate to Flora.

Ulysses leaped off Flora's shoulder and into her lap. He sniffed the plate.

"Our patient is hungry," said Dr. Meescham.

"He never had breakfast," said Flora. She took two sandwiches and handed one to Ulysses.

"This sofa," said Dr. Meescham, "is the sofa of my grandmother. She was born on this sofa. In Blundermeecen. She lived the whole of her life there. And she is buried there in a dark wood. But that is a different story.

"What I meant to say is that when I was a girl in Blundermeecen, I sat on this sofa and spoke with my grandmother about inconsequential things well into the gloom of the evening. That is what a girl in Blundermeecen did in those days. She was expected to speak of inconsequential things as the gloom of the evening descended. Also, she must knit. Always, the gloom was descending in Blundermeecen. Always, always one was knitting outfits for the little trolls."

"What little trolls?" said Flora. "And where's Blundermeecen?"

"Never mind about the trolls for now. I meant only to say that life was very gloomy then, and one was always knitting."

"It sounds lousy," said Flora.

"It was exactly this: lousy," said Dr. Meescham. She smiled. Her dentures were very bright; there was a smear of grape jelly on one of her fake incisors.

Flora reached for another sandwich. Had ***TERRIBLE THINGS CAN HAPPEN TO YOU!*** ever warned against eating jelly sandwiches in the house of a woman from Blundermeecen?

"Your father is a lonely man," said Dr. Meescham. "Also, very sad. To leave you, this broke his heart."

"It did?" said Flora.

"Yes, yes. Mr. George Buckman has sat on this horsehair sofa many times. He has talked of his sadness. He has wept. This sofa has seen the tears of many people. It is a sofa that is good for tears. They roll off it, you see."

Her father had sat on this couch and wept as the gloom of the evening descended?

Flora suddenly felt like she might cry, too. What was wrong with her?

Seal blubber, she thought. The words steadied her.

She handed another sandwich to Ulysses.

"Your father is very capacious of heart," said Dr. Meescham. "Do you know what this means?"

Flora shook her head.

"It means the heart of George Buckman is large. It is capable of containing much joy and much sorrow."

"Oh," said Flora.

For some reason, she heard William Spiver's voice saying that the universe was a random place.

"Capacious heart," said Dr. Meescham's voice.

"Random universe," said William Spiver's.

Capacious. Random. Heart. Universe.

Flora felt dizzy.

"I'm a cynic!" she announced for no particular reason and in a too-loud voice.

"Bah, cynics," said Dr. Meescham. "Cynics are people who are afraid to believe." She waved her hand in front of her face as if she were brushing away a fly.

"Do you believe in, um, things?" said Flora.

"Yes, yes, I believe," said Dr. Meescham. She smiled her too-bright smile again. "You have heard of Pascal's Wager?"

"No," said Flora.

"Pascal," said Dr. Meescham, "had it that since it could not be proven whether God existed, one might as well believe that he did, because there was everything to gain by believing and nothing to lose. This is how it is for me. What do I lose if I choose to believe? Nothing!

"Take this squirrel, for instance. Ulysses. Do I believe he can type poetry? Sure, I do believe it. There is much more beauty in the world if I believe such a thing is possible."

Flora and Dr. Meescham looked at Ulysses. He was holding half a sandwich in his front paws. There were blobs of grape jelly in his whiskers.

"Do you know what a superhero is?" said Flora.

"Sure, I know what a superhero is."

"Ulysses is a superhero," said Flora. "But he hasn't really done anything heroic yet. Mostly he's just flown around. He lifted a vacuum cleaner over his head. He wrote some poetry. He hasn't saved anyone, though. And that's what superheroes are supposed to do, save people."

"Who knows what he will do?" said Dr. Meescham. "Who knows whom he will save? So many miracles have not yet happened."

Flora watched as one of the jelly blobs on Ulysses's whiskers trembled and fell in slow motion to the horsehair sofa.

"All things are possible," said Dr. Meescham. "When I was a girl in Blundermeecen, the miraculous happened every day. Or every other day. Or every third day. Actually, sometimes it did not happen at all, even on the third day. But still, we expected it. You see what I'm saying? Even when it didn't happen, we were expecting it. We knew the miraculous would come."

There was a knock at the door.

"See?" said Dr. Meescham. "This will be your father, Mr. George Buckman."

Flora stood and went to the door and opened it. It was her father. And he was smiling. Again. Still. Which did seem kind of miraculous.

"Hi, Pop," she said.

"You see?" said Dr. Meescham. "He smiles."

Flora's father's smile got bigger. He took off his hat. He bowed. "George Buckman," he said. "How do you do?"

Flora couldn't help it; she smiled, too.

She was still smiling when a noise that sounded like the end of the world echoed through the hallway of the Blixen Arms. One minute her father was standing there with his hat in his hands, smiling, and the next minute, Mr. Klaus (the cat one) came out of nowhere and landed right on top of George Buckman's unprotected head.

CHAPTER FORTY
Vanquished!

AND THE SUPERHERO WAS ENORMOUSLY, INORDINATELY PLEASED WITH HIMSELF.

HE FELT IMMENSELY POWERFUL!

HE FELT LIKE WRITING A POEM!

CHAPTER FORTY-ONE
I Promise

They were in the car. Flora's father's hands were on the steering wheel at ten o'clock and two. Flora was sitting up front and Ulysses's head was out the window. They were heading back to Flora's mother's house in spite of Flora's protestations.

"We have to go back," said her father. "We have to return at the regular Saturday-afternoon time. We have to act normal, natural, unconcerned."

Flora wanted to object, but she could read the writing on the wall, or rather she could read the words that hovered above her and her father and the squirrel.

**DESTINY COULD NO LONGER BE FORESTALLED!
THE ARCH-NEMESIS MUST BE FACED!**

"Holy bagumba," said her father. His right ear was wrapped in a huge amount of gauze. His head looked lopsided. "Holy unanticipated occurrences! A squirrel vanquished a cat." He shook his head. He smiled.

"And now it's time for another battle," said Flora.

"Everything will be fine," said her father.

"So you say," said Flora.

It started to rain.

Ulysses pulled his head back inside the car. He looked up at Flora, and the sight of his little whiskered face calmed her somehow. She smiled at him, and the squirrel sighed happily and curled up in her lap.

"When I was a girl in Blundermeecen," Dr. Meescham had said to Flora when they were all leaving apartment 267, "we wondered always if we would see each other again. Each day was uncertain. So, to say good-bye to someone was uncertain, too. Would you see them again? Who could say? Blundermeecen was a place of dark secrets, unmarked graves, terrible curses. Trolls were everywhere! So we said good-bye to each other the best way we could. We said: I promise to always turn back toward you.

"I say those words to you now, Flora Belle. I promise to always turn back toward you. And now you must say them to me."

"I promise to always turn back toward you," Flora had said.

She whispered the words again, now, to the squirrel. "I promise to always turn back toward you."

She put a finger on Ulysses's chest. His tiny heart was beating out a message that felt like *I promise, I promise, I promise.*

Hearts were the strangest things.

"Pop?" said Flora.

"Yes," said her father.

"Can I feel your heart?"

"My heart?" said her father. "Okay. Sure."

And then, for the first time ever, George Buckman took both his hands off the steering wheel while the car was in motion. He opened his arms wide. Flora gently moved Ulysses out of her lap and onto the seat beside her, and then she reached up and across and put her hand on the left side of her father's chest.

And she felt it. Her father's heart, beating there inside of him. It felt very certain, very strong, and very large. Just like Dr. Meescham had said: capacious.

"Thank you," she told him.

"Sure," he said. "You bet."

He put his hands back on the steering wheel at ten o'clock and two, and the three of them—Flora, her father, and the squirrel—traveled the rest of the way home in a strange and peaceful silence.

The only noise was from the windshield wipers; they hummed back and forth, and back and forth, singing a sweet, out-of-tune song.

The squirrel slept.

And Flora Belle Buckman was happy.

CHAPTER FORTY-TWO
Foreboding

Her father pulled the car into the driveway and cut the engine. The windshield wipers let out a surprised squeak and then froze in midwave. The rain slowed to a trickle. The sun came out from behind a cloud and then disappeared again, and the smell of ketchup melded with butterscotch rose with a gentle persistence from the seats of the car.

"Here we are," said her father.

"Yep," said Flora. "Here we are."

412 Bellegrade Avenue.

It was the house that Flora had lived in for the whole of her life.

But something was different about it; something had changed.

What was it?

Ulysses crawled up onto her shoulder. She put her hand on him.

The house looked sneaky somehow, almost as if it were up to no good.

Foreboding.

That was the word that popped into Flora's head.

The house seemed full of foreboding.

"Do inanimate objects (couches, chairs, spatulas, etc.)

absorb the energy of the criminals, the wrongdoers among whom they live?" *The Criminal Element* had queried in a recent issue.

"It is, of course, entirely unscientific to assume such a thing. But still, we are forced to admit that in this woeful world, there exist objects with an almost palpable energy of menace . . . spatulas that seem cursed, couches that contain literal and metaphorical stains of the past, houses that seem to perpetually groan and moan for the sins contained in their environs. Can we explain this? No. Do we understand this? We do not. Do we know that criminals exist? We do. We are also terribly (and unfortunately) certain that the criminal element will be Forever Among Us."

And the arch-nemesis, thought Flora, *the arch-nemesis will be forever among us, too. Ulysses's arch-nemesis is in that house right now.*

"Do you remember the Darkness of 10,000 Hands?" Flora said to her father.

"Yep," said her father. "He wields 10,000 hands of anger, greed, and revenge. He is the sworn enemy of Incandesto."

"He's Incandesto's arch-nemesis," said Flora.

"Right," said her father. "I tell you what. The Darkness of 10,000 Hands better stay away from our squirrel."

He honked the horn.

"Home the warrior!" he shouted. "Home the cat-conquering, superhero squirrel!"

Ulysses puffed out his chest.

"Let's go," Flora said. "We have to do it. We have to face the arch-nemesis."

"Right!" said her father. "Bravely forward!"

And he honked the horn again.

CHAPTER FORTY-THREE
Treacle

They walked into the house, and the little shepherdess was waiting for them. She was standing where she always stood: the lamb at her feet, the tiny globe above her head, and a look on her face that said, *I know something you don't know.*

Flora's father took off his hat and bowed to the lamp. "George Buckman," he said. "How do you do?"

"Hello?" Flora shouted into the silence of the house.

From the kitchen came the sound of laughter.

"Mom?" said Flora.

No one answered.

Flora's sense of foreboding deepened, expanded.

And then her mother spoke.

She said, "That's absolutely right, William."

William?

William?

There was only one William that Flora knew. What would he be doing in the kitchen with a known arch-nemesis?

And then came the familiar rattle of the typewriter keys being struck, the thwack of the carriage return being hit.

Ulysses's grip on her shoulder tightened. He let out a small chirrup of excitement.

Her mother laughed again.

The laughter was followed by the truly terrifying words "Thank you so much, William."

"Shhh," said Flora to her father, who was standing, listening, his hat in his hands and a goofy smile on his face. There was a small, round drop of blood on his ear bandage. It looked oddly festive.

"You stay here," Flora said to him. "Ulysses and I will go and check this out."

"Right, right," said her father. "You bet. I'll stay here." He put his hat on his head. He nodded.

Flora, superhero on her shoulder, walked quietly, stealthily through the living room and into the dining room and stood before the closed kitchen door. She held herself very still. She made herself into a Giant Ear.

She was getting extremely good at making herself into a Giant Ear.

Flora listened, and she could feel Ulysses, his body tense and expectant, listening, too.

Her mother spoke. She said, "Yes, it will go like this: 'Frederico, I have dreamed of you for eons.'"

"No," said another voice, a high, thin, and extremely annoying voice. "'I've dreamed of you for all eternity.'"

"Ooooh," said Flora's mother. "'For all eternity.' That's good. More poetic."

Ulysses shifted his position on Flora's shoulder. He nodded.

"Yes, exactly," said William Spiver. "More poetic. 'Eons' sounds too geological. There's nothing romantic about geology, I assure you."

"Okay, okay," said Flora's mother. "Right. What's next, William?"

"Actually," said William Spiver, "if you don't mind, I would prefer to be called William Spiver."

"Of course," said Flora's mother. "I'm sorry. What's next, William Spiver?"

"Let me see," said William Spiver. "I suppose Frederico would say, 'And I have dreamed of you, Angelique. My darling! I must tell you that they were dreams so vivid and beautiful that I am loath to wake to reality.'"

"Ooooh, that's good. Hold on a sec."

The typewriter keys came to clacking life. The carriage return dinged.

"Do you think that's good?" Flora whispered to Ulysses. "Do you think that's good writing?"

Ulysses shook his head. His whiskers brushed against her cheek.

"I don't think so, either," she said.

Actually, she thought it was terrible. It was sickly sweet nonsense. There was a word for that. What was it?

Treacle. That was it.

Having located the correct word, Flora felt a sudden need to say the word aloud. And so she did. She pushed open the kitchen door. She stepped forward.

"Treacle!" she shouted.

"Flora?" said her mother.

"Treacle?" said William Spiver.

"Yes!" said Flora.

She was pleased that with one simple word she had answered two very important questions.

Yes, she was Flora.

And yes, it was treacle.

CHAPTER FORTY-FOUR
Her Treacherous Heart

William Spiver was wearing his dark glasses. There was a Pitzer Pop in his mouth. He was smiling.

He looked exactly like a villain.

That's what Flora's brain thought.

But her heart, her treacherous heart, rose up joyfully inside of her at the sight of him. Flora's heart was actually *glad* to see William Spiver.

There was so much she wanted to talk to him about: Pascal's Wager, Dr. Meescham, the other Dr. Meescham, giant squids, giant donuts (and who was dunking them), if he had ever heard of a place called Blundermeecen, if he had ever sat on a horsehair sofa.

But William Spiver was sitting beside Ulysses's arch-nemesis. Smiling.

Obviously he could not be trusted.

"Flora Belle?" said William Spiver.

"It's me," said Flora. "I'm surprised you don't smell me, William Spiver. Since you can smell everything."

"I have never claimed to be able to smell everything; however, it is true that right now I am smelling squirrel. And there is another odor. It is something sweet, some scent redolent of school lunchrooms on rainy Thursdays. What is it? Jelly. Yes, grape jelly. I smell squirrel and grape jelly."

"Squirrel?" said Flora's mother. She turned away from the typewriter. She looked at Flora. "Squirrel!" she said. "What in the world are you doing back here with that squirrel? I told your father—"

"This malfeasance must be stopped!" shouted Flora.

Her mother, hands still poised over the keys of the typewriter, stared at Flora with her mouth open.

William Spiver, for once, was silent.

On Flora's shoulder, the squirrel trembled.

Flora slowly raised her left arm. She pointed at her mother. She said, "What did you tell my father to do to the squirrel?"

Her mother cleared her throat. "I told your father—"

But the sentence remained unfinished, the truth unuttered, because the kitchen door suddenly swung open to reveal Flora's father.

"George Buckman," he said to the room at large. "How do you do?"

He walked into the kitchen. He stood beside Flora.

"George, what in the world?" said Flora's mother. "You look like you've been in a battle."

"I am fine, just fine. I was saved by the squirrel."

"What?" said Flora's mother.

"I was attacked by Mr. Klaus. He landed on my head. And—"

"This is fascinating," said William Spiver. "But may I interrupt for a moment?"

"Absolutely."

"Who is Mr. Klaus?"

"Mr. Klaus is a landlord and also a cat. A large cat. Usually he attacks ankles. This time it was the head. My head. It was a very surprising attack. I wasn't prepared."

"And?" said William Spiver.

"Oh, yes. And. And Mr. Klaus bit my ear. And there was a lot of pain. And the squirrel rescued me."

"Have. You. Lost. Your. Mind?" said Flora's mother.

"I don't think so," said Flora's father. He smiled hopefully.

"Can't you handle the smallest task? I asked you to take care of the squirrel situation."

Flora felt a wave of anger roll through her. "Quit speaking euphemistically," she said. "Quit calling it 'the squirrel situation.' You asked him to kill. You asked him to murder my squirrel!"

Ulysses let out a chirp of agreement.

And then the kitchen became as silent as the tomb.

CHAPTER FORTY-FIVE
Four Words

"It's the truth," Flora said. "You told Pop to kill Ulysses."

Having denounced her mother, Flora now turned her attention to William Spiver and his betrayal.

"What are you even doing here, William Spiver? Why are you in the kitchen? With my mother?"

"He's assisting me with my novel."

William Spiver blushed a bright and otherworldly red. "I'm delighted that you find me of some assistance, Mrs. Buckman," he said. He took the Pitzer Pop out of his mouth and bowed in the direction of Flora's mother. "I must admit that I have always had a certain facility with words. And I am terribly fond of the novel form. Though my interests lie less in the area of romance and more in the speculative nature of things. Science fiction, if you will. Fact blended with fantasy, an extended meditation on the nature of the universe. Quarks, dwarf stars, black holes, and the like. Do you know, for instance, that the universe is expanding as we speak?"

Only Ulysses responded to this question. The squirrel shook his head vigorously, obviously amazed.

William Spiver pushed his dark glasses up higher on his nose. He took a deep breath. "Speaking of expansion, did you know that there are now something like ninety billion galaxies in the universe? In such a universe, it seems ridiculous and foolhardy to attempt a creation of one's own, but still, I persevere. I persevere."

"You didn't answer my question, William Spiver," said Flora.

"Let me try again," he said.

"No," said Flora. "You're a traitor. And you"—she wheeled and pointed at her mother—"are an arch-nemesis, a true villain."

Flora's mother crossed her arms. She said, "I'm someone who wants what's best for you. If that makes me a villain, fine."

Flora took a deep breath. "I'm moving in with Pop," she said.

"What?" said her mother.

"Really?" said her father.

"Your father," said her mother, "doesn't know how to take care of himself, much less someone else."

"At least he doesn't wish he had a lamp for a daughter," said Flora.

"I feel like I'm missing something," said William Spiver.

"I want to live with Pop," said Flora.

"Really?" said her father again.

"Go right ahead," said her mother. "It would certainly make my life easier."

Make my life easier.

Those four words (so small, so simple, so ordinary) came

flying at Flora like enormous slabs of stone. She actually felt herself tip sideways as they hit her. She put up a hand and held on to Ulysses. She used the squirrel to steady herself.

"Do not hope," she whispered. But she wasn't sure what it was that she wasn't hoping for.

All she knew was that she was a cynic, and her heart hurt. Cynics' hearts weren't supposed to hurt.

William Spiver pushed back his chair. He stood. "Mrs. Buckman," he said, "perhaps you would like to retract those last words? They seem unnecessarily harsh."

Flora's mother said nothing.

William Spiver remained standing. "Okay, then," he said. "I will speak. I will attempt, yet again, to make myself clear." He paused. "The only reason I am here, Flora Belle, is that I came looking for you. You were gone a long time and I missed you, and I wondered if you had returned and I came to find you."

Flora closed her eyes. She saw nothing but darkness. And into this darkness slowly swam the other Dr. Meescham's giant squid, moving sadly along, flailing its eight lonely and enormous arms.

I came to find you.

What was it with William Spiver and the words he said to her? Why did they make her heart squinch up?

"Seal blubber," said Flora.

"I beg your pardon?" said William Spiver.

Ulysses gently pushed against Flora's hand.

And then the squirrel leaped away from her.

"Oh, no," said Flora's mother. "No. Not that. No, no . . ."

Ulysses flew over Phyllis Buckman's head. He went high and then higher still.

"Yes," said Flora. "Yes."

CHAPTER FORTY-SIX
Gianter

CHAPTER FORTY-SEVEN
Flying Squirrels

Why, Flora wondered, did everything become silent when Ulysses flew?

It had been the same in the Giant Do-Nut (at least until everyone started screaming). It was as if some small peace descended. The world became dreamy, beautiful, slow.

Flora looked around her. She smiled. The sun was shining into the kitchen, illuminating everything: Ulysses's whiskers, the typewriter keys, her father's upturned and smiling face, and her mother's astonished and disbelieving one.

Even William Spiver was illuminated, his white hair glowing like a wild halo.

"What is it?" said William Spiver. "What's going on?"

Flora's father laughed. "Do you see, Phyllis? Do you? Anything can happen."

Ulysses floated above them. He zoomed down to the ground and then went shooting back up to the ceiling. He looked behind him and performed a lazy, midair backflip.

"For the love of Pete," said Flora's mother in a strange and wooden voice.

"Someone tell me something," said William Spiver.

Ulysses dived down again. He flew past William Spiver's right ear.

"Acccck," said William Spiver. "What was that?"

"The squirrel," said Flora's mother in her strange, new voice. "He is flying." She stood up suddenly. "Right," she said. "Okay. I have to go upstairs and take a nap."

Which was an odd thing for her to say because Flora's mother was not, in any way, a napper. In fact, she was an anti-napper. She didn't believe in naps at all. She often said that they were a big, fat waste of time.

"Yes, a little nap. That is what I need."

Flora's mother walked out of the kitchen and closed the door behind her.

Ulysses landed on the table next to the typewriter.

"It's not *that* shocking," said William Spiver. "There are flying squirrels, you know. They exist. In fact, there are some theories that posit that all squirrels are descended from the flying squirrel. In any case, flying squirrels themselves are a documented fact."

Ulysses looked at William Spiver and then over at Flora.

He reached out a paw and hit a key on the typewriter.

The single *clack* echoed through the kitchen.

"How about flying squirrels who type?" said Flora.

"Not as well documented," admitted William Spiver.

Ulysses hit another key. And then another.

"Holy bagumba," said Flora's father. "He flies. He vanquishes cats. And he types."

"He's a superhero," said Flora.

"It's amazing," said her father. "It's wonderful. But I think I better go have a quick word with your mother about the whole, um, situation."

CHAPTER FORTY-EIGHT
Banished

Clack . . . clack . . . clack.

Flora stood silently.

William Spiver stood silently.

The squirrel typed.

"Flora Belle?" said William Spiver.

"Uh-huh?" said Flora.

"I wanted to make sure you were still here."

"Where else would I be?"

"Well, I don't know. You did say that you were moving out."

"My mother wants me to leave," said Flora.

"I don't know if that's exactly what she meant," said William Spiver. "I think she was surprised. And perhaps her feelings were hurt. She certainly didn't express herself very well. Shocking, really, that a romance novelist could be so inept at the language of the heart."

Clack . . . clack . . . clack.

Ulysses had a look of deep and supreme satisfaction on his face.

"She said it would be easier without me," said Flora.

"Yes, well," said William Spiver. He pushed his glasses back up on his nose. He pulled out a chair and sat down again at the kitchen table. He sighed a deep sigh.

"My lips are numb," said Flora.

"I know that feeling," said William Spiver. "Having suffered through several traumatic episodes myself, I am very familiar with the bodily manifestations of grief."

"What happened to you?" asked Flora.

"I was banished."

Banished.

It was a word that Flora could feel in the pit of her stomach, a small, cold stone of a word.

"Why were you banished?"

"I think the more relevant question would be: Who banished me?"

"Okay," said Flora. "Who banished you?"

"My mother," said William Spiver.

Flora felt another stone fall to the bottom of her stomach.

"Why?" she said.

"There was an unfortunate incident involving my mother's new husband, a man who is not my father. A man who bears the idiotic appellation Tyrone."

"Where's your father?" said Flora.

"He died."

"Oh."

One more stone sank to the bottom of Flora's stomach.

"My father, my real father, was a man of great humanity and intelligence," said William Spiver. "Also, he had delicate feet. Very, very tiny feet. I, too, am small of foot."

Flora looked at William Spiver's feet. They did seem extremely small.

"Not that that is particularly relevant information. In any case, my father was a man who could play the piano wonderfully well. He had an in-depth knowledge of astronomy. He liked to consider the stars. His name was William.

"But he's dead. And now my mother is married to a man named Tyrone, who does not have delicate feet and who is supremely unaware that there are stars in the sky. The mysteries of the universe mean nothing to him. He sold my father's piano. He is a man who refuses to call me William. Instead, this man refers to me as Billy.

"My name, as you know, is not now, nor has it ever been, nor will it ever be, Billy. I took issue with being so addressed. I repeatedly took issue. And after repeatedly taking issue and repeatedly being ignored, one thing led to another and some irrevocable acts occurred. And thus, I was banished."

"What thing led to another thing?" said Flora. "What irrevocable acts occurred?"

"It's complicated," said William Spiver. "I don't want to talk about it right now. But as long as we are asking each other questions of an emotionally fraught nature, why did you say that your mother wanted a lamp for a daughter?"

"It's complicated," said Flora.

"I'm certain that it is. And I empathize."

There was another long silence punctuated by the clacking of typewriter keys.

"The squirrel is working on another poem, I suppose," said William Spiver.

"I guess," said Flora.

"It sounds like a long one. Epic in nature. What in the world would a squirrel have to write about at such length?"

"A lot happened today," said Flora.

It was late afternoon. The shadows of the elm and the maple in the backyard entered the kitchen and flung themselves in purple lines across the floor.

Flora would miss those shadows when she moved away.

She would miss the trees.

She supposed she would even miss William Spiver.

And then, almost as if he were reading her mind, William Spiver said, "I meant what I said. I'm here because I was looking for you. I missed you."

Flora's heart, the lonely, many-armed squid of it, flipped and flailed inside of her.

She opened her mouth to say that it didn't matter, not really, not now. But as usual, what she intended to say to William Spiver and what she said were two different things.

The sentence Flora intended to say was "It doesn't matter."

The sentence she said was "Have you ever heard of a place called Blundermeecen?"

"Pardon me," said William Spiver. He held up his right hand. "I don't mean to alarm you. But do you smell smoke?"

Flora sniffed. She did smell smoke.

Now there was going to be a fire? On top of everything else?

For the love of Pete.

CHAPTER FORTY-NINE
Good News, Flora Belle!

Flora's mother and father entered the kitchen together. Her mother had a cigarette in her mouth.

Her mother was smoking!

Her father had his arm around her mother's shoulder.

This was almost as alarming as seeing her mother smoke. Her mother and father never touched anymore.

"Good news, Flora Belle!" said her father.

"Really?" said Flora.

She never believed it when someone said there was good news. In her experience, when there was good news, people just said what the good news was. If there was bad news that they wanted you to believe was good news, then they said, "Good news!"

And if there was really bad news, they said, "Good news, Flora Belle!"

"Your mother thinks that it would be wonderful to have the squirrel stay here," said her father.

"What?" said Flora. "Here? With her? And where am I supposed to stay?"

"Here," said her father. "With your mother. You, your mother, and the squirrel. That's what your mother would like."

Flora looked at her mother. "Mom?" she said.

“I would be honored,” said her mother. She took a long drag on her cigarette. Her hand was trembling.

“Why are you smoking?” said Flora. “I thought you stopped smoking.”

“It seemed like the wrong time to stop,” said her mother. She squinted. “I am under a lot of pressure right now. Speaking of which, I see that the squirrel is typing. On my typewriter. Where I write.”

“He writes poetry,” said William Spiver, “not fiction.”

“Let’s just have a look-see,” said Flora’s mother. She walked over to the typewriter and stood looking down at Ulysses and at the words on the page. “Let’s see what kind of poetry a squirrel types.”

Her voice sounded funny still, tinny and far away, as if she were speaking from the bottom of a dark well. Actually, what she sounded like was a robot, someone pretending to be human and doing a lousy job of it.

Flora felt a little flicker of fear.

“Let me just light another cigarette here,” said her mother in her robot voice.

She lit a new cigarette from the tip of the old one, which was, of course, chain-smoking and dangerous behavior at the best of times.

And this, obviously, was not the best of times.

Her mother inhaled deeply on the cigarette. She exhaled. She said, “Shall I read the squirrel poetry aloud?”

CHAPTER FIFTY
An Incomplete List

Actually, it wasn't poetry.

Not yet.

So far, it was just a list of words that he wanted to turn into a poem.

The first word on the list was `Jelly`.

`Jelly` was followed by **`Giant donut`**, which was, in turn, followed by `Sprinkle`.

The list continued on with these words:

`RITA!`

`Sunny-side up`

`Pascal`

`Giant squid`

`Little shepherdess`

`Vanquished`

`Capacious`

`Quark`

`Universe (expanding)`

`Blundermeecen`

`Banished`

The list ended with the words of Dr. Meescham's good-bye:

`I promise to always turn back`

`toward you.`

The words were good words, Ulysses felt, maybe even great words, but the list was very incomplete. He was just getting started. The words needed to be arranged, fussed with, put in the order of his heart.

All of this is to say that when Flora's mother read the list out loud, it didn't sound terribly impressive.

"Gosh, that's some swell poetry," said George Buckman.

"Not really," said William Spiver. "There's no point in lying to him, even if he is a squirrel. It's actually pretty lousy poetry. But I do like the last part, the part about turning back. That has some emotional heft to it."

"Well, I think it is just great," said Flora's mother. "And I'm glad to welcome another writer into the family."

She patted Ulysses on the head. Too forcefully, he felt. The pat approached violence.

"We are going to be one happy little family," said Flora's mother. She gave Ulysses another whack disguised as a pat.

"Really?" said Flora.

"Oh, yes," said Flora's mother.

There was a knock at the back door. "Yoo-hoo," someone called out.

Tootie! thought Ulysses.

"Tootie!" said Flora.

"Mrs. Tickham," said Flora's mother. "Do come in. We were just reading some words that the squirrel typed. Ha-ha. We were reading some squirrel poetry."

"William," said Tootie, "I've been calling and calling you."

"I didn't hear you."

"Well, I must admit that I wasn't calling very loudly," said Tootie. "What did Ulysses type?"

Flora's mother read the list of words again.

Tootie put her hand over her heart and said, "Oh, those last lines are beautiful, heartbreaking."

"Those last lines are the only bit of coherence in the whole thing," said William Spiver.

"I've been inspired by Ulysses to write a little poetry of my own," said Tootie.

Ulysses felt himself puff up. He had inspired Tootie! He turned and sniffed his tail.

"I'd like to read your poetry, Tootie," said Flora.

"Well, we should have a poetry reading at some point. I'm sure Ulysses would enjoy that."

The squirrel nodded.

Yes, yes. He would enjoy that.

He would also enjoy a bite to eat.

Dr. Meescham's jelly sandwiches had been wonderful, but that was a long time ago. He would like to eat, and he would like for Tootie to read poetry to him. And he would like to work on his own poem.

Also, he would like for Flora's mother to quit pounding him on the head, which she was doing again now.

"William," said Tootie, "your mother called for you."

"Did she?" said William Spiver. His voice was squeaky with hope. "Really? Did she ask for me to come home?"

"Unfortunately not," said Tootie. "But it's dinnertime. Come home with me and eat something."

Home, thought Ulysses. *That's a good word. And* dinner *is a good word, too.*

He turned back to the typewriter.

He searched for the *H.*

CHAPTER FIFTY-ONE
Possessed!

Things were very strange.

Her mother insisted that they sit together at the dining-room table. The three of them. She also insisted that Ulysses sit in a chair, which was ridiculous, because if he sat in a chair, he wouldn't be able to reach the table.

"He can sit here, with me," said Flora.

"Oh, no, no. I want him to feel welcome. I want him to know that he literally has a chair at our table."

Her mother had held the chair out and Ulysses had climbed onto it, and then she slid the chair all the way under the table. It was enough to break your heart, watching his whiskered, hopeful face as it disappeared beneath the tablecloth.

If her mother hadn't been acting so strange, Flora would have said something, would have argued more vehemently.

But her mother *was* acting strange.

Very, very strange.

Not only was her voice robotic; she was also saying things that she never would have said before, expressing sentiments that seemed to be at odds with the mother Flora had always known.

For instance: wanting a squirrel to have a chair at the table.

For instance: encouraging Flora to have a second helping of macaroni and cheese.

For instance: saying nothing about Flora's potential stoutness as Flora consumed the second helping of macaroni and cheese.

It was almost as if her mother were possessed.

TERRIBLE THINGS CAN HAPPEN TO YOU! had done an issue entitled "Devils, Dybbuks, and Curses." Apparently, throughout history, people who acted strange had been accused of being inhabited by the devil or a demon. Or an alien from outer space. According to **TERRIBLE THINGS!**, these people were (most likely) not possessed. Rather, their psyches had been pushed by extraordinary events to the breaking point, and they had experienced a sort of nervous collapse.

Flora's guess was that a typing, flying squirrel was more (much more) than Flora's mother's psyche could manage. She had been pushed to the brink. She was suffering from some kind of nervous breakdown.

Either that or she was possessed.

Of course, Flora's father had been pushed to the brink, too. But everything to do with Ulysses had affected him differently. It had cheered him up somehow, maybe because the holy-bagumba-ness of it all had reminded him of Incandesto and Dolores and, also, of the possibility of impossible things.

"Can't I come live with you?" Flora had said to her father when he left that night.

"Absolutely you can come live with me," said her father. "But your mother needs you now."

"She doesn't need me," said Flora. "She said that her life would be easier without me."

"I think that your mother has forgotten how to say what she means," said her father.

"Plus," said Flora, "she hates Ulysses. I can't live with someone who hates my squirrel."

"Give her a chance," said her father.

"Right," said Flora.

As her father left the house that night, Flora had whispered the words of Dr. Meescham's good-bye to him, and even though there was no way he could hear her, Flora was disappointed when her father didn't turn around, back toward her.

But, anyway, here she was, giving her mother a chance, which, as far as Flora could tell, meant watching Phyllis Buckman use the candle on the dining-room table to light cigarette after cigarette.

Flora fully expected that at some point, her mother's hair would catch on fire.

What did you do when somebody's hair caught fire? It had something to do with a throw rug. You beat them over the head with a throw rug—that was it. Flora looked around the dining room. Did they even own a throw rug?

She caught sight of the little shepherdess standing at the bottom of the stairs. Mary Ann was looking at Flora and her mother with a jaded and judgmental eye. For once, Flora agreed with the lamp: things were out of control.

Her mother said, "Well, it is such a delight to spend time with the members of my family, rodent and otherwise. But my head hurts, and I think that I will go upstairs and rest my eyes for a while."

"Okay," said Flora. "I'll clear the table."

"Lovely. So very thoughtful."

After her strange mother climbed the stairs, Flora pulled back Ulysses's chair. He hopped up on the table and considered the plate full of macaroni and cheese. He looked at Flora.

"Go ahead," she said. "It's for you."

He picked up a single noodle and held it in his paws, admiring it.

Watching him, Flora suddenly remembered a panel from ***The Illuminated Adventures of the Amazing Incandesto!*** It was a picture of Alfred T. Slipper standing at a darkened window. His hands were behind his back and Dolores was on his shoulder, and Alfred was looking out the window and saying, "I am alone in the world, Dolores, and I am homesick for my own kind."

The squirrel ate the noodle and picked up another one. There was cheese sauce on his whiskers. He looked happy.

"I'm homesick," said Flora. "I miss my father."

Ulysses looked up at her.

"I miss William Spiver."

Talk about a sentence you could never predict you would say.

I even miss my mother, thought Flora, *or I miss the person she used to be.*

It was dark outside.

Her mother was upstairs. Her father was at the Blixen Arms. William Spiver was next door.

The universe was expanding.

And Flora Belle Buckman was homesick for her own kind.

CHAPTER FIFTY-TWO
Is There a Word for That?

He sat in the window of Flora's room and looked down at the sleeping Flora and then up and out, at the lighted windows of the other houses. He thought about the words he would like to add to his poem. He thought about the music at Dr. Meescham's house, the way the voices sounded, singing. He thought about the look on Mr. Klaus's face when he went sailing backward down the hallway.

Was there a word for that?

Was there a word for all those things together? The lighted windows and the music and the terrified, disbelieving look on a cat's face when he was vanquished?

The squirrel listened to the wind blowing through the leaves on the trees. He closed his eyes and imagined a giant donut with sprinkles on top of it and cream inside of it. Or jelly, maybe.

He thought about flying.

He thought about the look on Flora's face when her mother said that life would be easier without her.

What was a squirrel supposed to do with all of these thoughts and feelings?

Flora let out a small snore.

Ulysses opened his eyes. He kept them open until the lights in the windows of the other houses went off one by one, and the world went dark except for a single streetlight at the end of the block. The streetlight fizzled into darkness and then flared back to life and then fizzled again . . . darkness; light; darkness; light.

What, Ulysses wondered, *does the streetlight want to say?*

He thought about William Spiver.

He thought about the word *banished* and the word *homesick.*

He imagined typing the words and watching them appear on the paper, letter by letter.

Flora had told him before she went to sleep that she thought it would be a good idea if he didn't type anything for a while, at least not on her mother's typewriter.

"It seems to provoke her," she said. "I think your typing poems and flying around the kitchen kind of made her have a nervous collapse. Or something."

She had said this, and then she had given him a sad look and closed the door to the bedroom. "I closed the door as a reminder, okay? No typewriter. No typing."

BUT WHAT WAS A CLOSED DOOR TO A SUPERHERO?
YOU STUPID LITTLE SHEPHERDESS.
IT WAS SUPERHERO TIME!
OR SOMETHING.

CHAPTER FIFTY-THREE
A Sign

Flora was dreaming.

She was sitting on the bank of a river. William Spiver was sitting beside her. The sun was shining, and a long way off, there was a sign, a neon sign. There was a word on the sign, but Flora couldn't read it.

"What does the sign say?" Flora asked.

"What sign?" said William Spiver. "I'm temporarily blind."

It was comforting to have William Spiver act just as annoying in a dream as he would in real life. Flora relaxed. She stared at the river. She had never seen anything so bright.

"If I were an explorer and I discovered this river, I would call it the Incandesto," said Flora.

"Think of the universe as an accordion," said William Spiver.

Flora felt a prick of irritation. "What does that mean?" she said.

"Can't you hear it?" asked William Spiver. He tilted his head to one side. He listened.

Flora listened, too. It sounded as if someone a long way off were playing a toy piano.

"Isn't it beautiful?" said William Spiver.

"It doesn't sound much like an accordion to me," said Flora.

"Oh, Flora Belle," said William Spiver, "you're so cynical. Of course it's an accordion."

The sign was closer. It had moved somehow. The neon letters were blinking on and off and on and off, spelling out the words WELCOME TO BLUNDERMEECEN.

"Wow," said Flora.

"What?" said William Spiver.

"I can read the sign."

"What does it say?"

"Welcome to Blundermeecen," said Flora.

The piano music got louder. William Spiver took hold of her hand. They sat together on the banks of the Incandesto River, and Flora was perfectly happy.

She thought, *I don't feel homesick at all.*

She thought, *William Spiver is holding my hand!*

And then she thought, *I wonder where Ulysses is.*

CHAPTER FIFTY-FOUR
Dear Flora

The kitchen was dark, lit only by the light above the stove. The squirrel was alone. But he had the strange feeling of not being alone. It was almost as if a cat were watching him.

Had Mr. Klaus tracked him down? Was he hiding in the shadows, waiting to exact his revenge? Cat revenge was a terrible thing. Cats never forgot an insult. Never. And to be thrown down a hallway (backward) by a squirrel was a terrible insult.

Ulysses held himself very still. He put his nose up in the air and sniffed, but he didn't smell cat.

He smelled smoke.

Flora's mother stepped out of the shadows and into the muted light of the kitchen.

"So," she said, "I see you helped yourself to my typewriter again, put your little squirrel paws all over it." She took another step forward. She put the cigarette in her mouth and reached out with both hands and yanked the paper from the typewriter.

The rollers screamed in protest.

Flora's mother crumpled the poem (without looking at it, without reading one word of it) and dropped the paper on the floor.

"So," she said.

She exhaled a ring of smoke, and the circle floated in the dim light of the kitchen, a beautiful, mysterious O. As he considered the cigarette smoke suspended in the air above him, Ulysses felt a wave of joy and sorrow, both things at once.

He loved the world. He loved all of it: smoke rings and lonely squids and giant donuts and Flora Belle Buckman's round head and all the wonderful thoughts inside of it. He loved William Spiver and his expanding universe. He loved Mr. George Buckman and his hat and the way he looked when he laughed. He loved Dr. Meescham and her watery eyes and her jelly sandwiches. He loved Tootie, who had called him a poet. He loved the stupid little shepherdess. He even loved Mr. Klaus.

He loved the world, this world; he didn't want to leave.

Flora's mother reached past him and picked up a blank piece of paper and rolled it into the typewriter.

"You want to type?" she said.

He nodded. He did want to type. He loved typing.

"Okay, let's type. You are going to type what I say."

But that went against the whole point of typing, typing what someone else said.

"Dear Flora," said Flora's mother.

Ulysses shook his head.

"Dear Flora," said Flora's mother again in a louder, more insistent voice.

Ulysses looked up at her. Smoke exited her nostrils in two thin streams.

"Do it," she said.

Slowly, slowly, the squirrel typed the words.

Dear Flora,

And then, stunned into a dumb willingness, he typed every terrible, untrue word that came out of Phyllis Buckman's mouth.

The squirrel took dictation.

CHAPTER FIFTY-FIVE
A Stone Squirrel

When he was finished, Flora's mother stood over his shoulder, reading and nodding and saying, "That's right, that's right. That ought to do it. There are a few misspellings. But then, you're a squirrel. Of course you're going to misspell things."

She lit another cigarette and leaned against the kitchen table and considered him. "I guess it's time," she said. "Wait here. I'll be right back."

And he did as she said. He waited.

She left the kitchen, and he simply sat there, unmoving. It was as if she had put a spell on him; it was as if typing the lies, the wrong words, had depleted him of all ability to act.

Once, long ago, in a garden in springtime, Ulysses had seen a squirrel made of stone: gray, hollow eyed, frozen. In his stone paws, he held a stone acorn that he would never get to consume. That squirrel was probably in the garden now, still holding that acorn, still waiting.

I am a stone squirrel, thought Ulysses. *I can't move.*

He looked over at the words he had typed. They were untrue words. Several of them were misspelled. There was no joy in them, no love. And worst of all, they were words that would hurt Flora.

He turned slowly. He sniffed his tail. And as he sniffed, he remembered the words that Flora had shouted at him in the Giant Do-Nut. "Remember who you are! You're Ulysses."

This helpful advice had been followed by a single, powerful word: "Act."

He heard the sound of footsteps.

What should he do? What action should he take?

He should type.

He should type a word.

But what word?

CHAPTER FIFTY-SIX
Kidnapped!

She woke with a start. The house was incredibly dark, so dark that Flora wondered if she had gone temporarily blind.

"Ulysses?" she said.

She sat up and stared in the direction of the door. Slowly the rectangular outline of it appeared, and then she could see that it was ajar.

"Ulysses?" she said again.

She got out of bed and went down the darkened stairs and past the little shepherdess.

"You stupid lamp," she said.

She made her way into the kitchen. It was empty. The typewriter was unmanned. Or unsquirreled.

"Ulysses?" said Flora.

She walked over to the typewriter and saw a piece of paper glowing white in the dim light.

"Uh-oh," she said.

She leaned in close. She squinted.

Dear Flora, I am teribly fond of you. But I here the call of the wild. And I must return to my natrual habitat. Thank you for the macroni and cheese. Yours, Mr. Squirrel.

Mr. Squirrel?

Call of the wild?

Teribly fond?

It was the biggest lie that Flora had ever read in her life. It didn't look like Ulysses had written it at all.

Only at the very end did the truth appear. Two letters: *F* and *L*. That was Ulysses, she knew, trying to type her name one last time, trying to tell her that he loved her.

"I love you, too," she whispered to the paper.

And then she looked around the kitchen. What kind of cynic was she, whispering "I love you" to a squirrel who wasn't even there?

But she did love him. She loved his whiskers. She loved his words. She loved his happiness, his little head, his determined heart, his nutty breath. She loved how beautiful he looked when he flew.

She felt her heart seize up. Why hadn't she told him that? She should have said those words to him.

But that didn't matter now. What mattered was finding him. Flora hadn't been reading ***The Criminal Element*** for two solid years for nothing. She knew what was going on. The squirrel had been kidnapped. By her mother!

She took a deep breath. She considered what to do, what action to take.

"In the event of a true and genuine emergency, an

absolute and undeniable crime, the authorities must be notified immediately," said *The Criminal Element.*

Flora was certain that this was a true and genuine emergency, an absolute and undeniable crime.

Still, it didn't seem like a good idea to notify the authorities.

If she called the police, what would she say?

My mother kidnapped my squirrel?

The Criminal Element: "If for some reason the authorities are not accessible to you, then you must seek help in other quarters. Whom do you trust? Whom do you know to be a safe port in a storm?"

Flora suddenly remembered her dream, how warm William Spiver's hand had felt in her own.

She blushed.

Whom did she trust?

Good grief, she trusted William Spiver.

CHAPTER FIFTY-SEVEN
Tootie to the Rescue

It was 2:20 a.m.

The grass was heavy with dew. Flora was picking her way through the darkness. She was breathing heavily because she was carrying Mary Ann in her arms, and Mary Ann — for all of her pink cheeks and delicate features and excessive, stupid frilliness — was incredibly heavy.

Talk about stout, thought Flora.

The Criminal Element: "Can one reason with a criminal? This is debatable. But it is true that the rules of nursery school are often in good effect in the criminal world. What do we mean by this? We mean that if the criminal has something you want, then you must have something he wants. Only then is it possible for some kind of 'discussion' to begin."

There was nothing and no one that Flora's mother loved more than the lamp. Together, Flora and William Spiver would find her mother. They would offer to exchange the little shepherdess for the squirrel. And then all would be well. Or something.

That was Flora's plan.

But first she had to find William Spiver, and she didn't think that it would be a good idea to ring Tootie's doorbell at 2:20 a.m.

"William Spiver?" said Flora.

Here she was, standing in the dark holding an unlit lamp and hoping that a temporarily blind boy would hear her call his name and come help her rescue her squirrel (a squirrel who, for a superhero, sure did seem to need a lot of rescuing).

Things were pretty grim.

"William Spiver?" she said again. "William Spiver."

And then, without really intending to, she started saying William Spiver's name over and over, louder and louder.

"WilliamSpiverWilliamSpiverWilliamSpiverWilliamSpiver WILLIAMSPIVERWILLIAMSPIVER."

There was no way he would be able to hear her, of course. She knew that. But she couldn't make herself stop. She just stupidly, idiotically, hopefully, kept saying his name.

"Flora Belle?"

"WilliamSpiverWilliamSpiverWilliamSpiver."

"Flora Belle?"

"WilliamSpiverWilliamSpiverWilliamSpiver."

"FLORA BELLE!"

And there he was, standing at a darkened window, conjured, apparently, by her need and her desperation. And her words.

William Spiver.

Or at least the shadow of William Spiver.

"Oh," said Flora, "hello."

"Yes, hello to you, too," said William Spiver. "How lovely of you to visit in the middle of the night."

"There's been an emergency," said Flora.

"Right," said William Spiver. "Just let me put on my bathrobe."

Flora felt a familiar prick of irritation. "It's an emergency, William Spiver. There's no time to waste. Forget about your bathrobe."

"I'll just put on my bathrobe," said William Spiver as if she hadn't said anything at all, "and I'll be right there. Wherever *there* is. It is shockingly difficult to locate even the most obvious things when one is temporarily blind. The world is very hard to navigate when you can't see.

"Although to be perfectly frank, I had trouble navigating the world even before the advent of the blindness. I've never been what you would call coordinated or spatially intelligent. It's not even that I bump into things. It's more that things leap out of nowhere and bump into me. My mother says that this is because I live in my head as opposed to living in the world. But I ask you: Don't we all live in our heads? Where else could we possibly exist? Our brains *are* the universe. Don't you think that's true? Flora Belle?"

"I said it's an emergency!"

"Well, then, I'll just put on my bathrobe, and we'll sort it all out."

Flora put Mary Ann down on the ground. She looked around wildly in the darkness. What was she looking for? She didn't know. Maybe a stick that she could use to hit William Spiver over the head.

"Flora Belle?"

"Ulysses is gone!" she screamed. "My mother kidnapped him. I think my mother is possessed. I think she might hurt him."

Do not cry, she told herself. *Do not cry. Do not hope. Do not cry. Just observe.*

"Shhh," said William Spiver. "It's okay, Flora Belle. I'll help you. We'll find him."

And then the light in William Spiver's room came on, and Tootie said, "What in the world are you doing, William?"

"Looking for my bathrobe."

TOOTIE TO THE RESCUE!

The words appeared above Tootie's head in a neon kind of brightness.

"Tootie," shouted Flora, "it's an emergency! My mother has kidnapped the squirrel."

"Flora?" said Tootie. She stuck her head out the window. "Why do you have that awful lamp?"

"It's complicated," said Flora.

"Again with the lamp?" said William Spiver. "What in the world is the meaning of the lamp?"

"My mother loves the lamp," said Flora. "I'm holding it hostage."

"Desperate times call for desperate measures," said Tootie.

"That's right," said Flora. "It's an emergency."

"I'll just get my purse," said Tootie.

CHAPTER FIFTY-EIGHT
Nothing Personal

It was dark — very, very dark.

And there was the smell of smoke.

Flora's mother had him in a sack and the sack was flung over her back, and she was walking somewhere and it was very, very dark. At the last minute, Flora's mother had picked up the piece of paper with his poem on it and thrown it into the sack along with him.

Was this meant as a kindness?

Was she mocking him?

Or was she merely covering her tracks?

The squirrel didn't know, but he held the crumpled ball of paper to his chest and tried to comfort himself. He thought, *Worse things have happened to me.*

He tried to think of what they were.

There was the time the pickup truck had run over his tail. That had hurt very much. There was also the incident with the BB gun. And the teddy bear. And the garden hose. The sling-shot. The bow and (rubber) arrow.

But everything that had happened before paled in comparison to this because there was so much more to lose now: Flora and her round and lovable head. Cheese puffs. Poetry. Giant donuts.

Shoot! He was going to leave the world without ever having tried a giant donut.

And Tootie! Tootie had said that she was going to read poetry out loud to him. That would never happen now, either.

It was very dark in the sack.

It was very dark everywhere.

I'm going to die, thought the squirrel. He hugged his poem closer, and the paper crackled and sighed.

"This is nothing personal, Mr. Squirrel," said Flora's mother.

Ulysses held himself very still. He found this sentiment difficult to believe.

"It really has nothing to do with you," said Flora's mother. "It's about Flora. Flora Belle. She is a strange child. And the world is not kind to the strange. She was strange before, and she's stranger now. Now she is walking around with a squirrel on her shoulder. Talking to a squirrel. Talking to a typing, flying squirrel. Not good. Not good at all."

Was Flora strange?

He supposed so.

But what was wrong with that?

She was strange in a good way. She was strange in a lovable way. Her heart was so big. It was capacious. Just like George Buckman's heart.

"Do you know what I want?" said Flora's mother.

Ulysses couldn't imagine.

"I want things to be normal. I want a daughter who is happy.

I want her to have friends who aren't squirrels. I don't want her to end up unloved and all alone in the world. But it doesn't matter, does it?"

It does matter, thought Ulysses.

"It's time to do what needs to be done," said Flora's mother.

She stopped walking.

Uh-oh, thought Ulysses.

CHAPTER FIFTY-NINE
Destination Unknown

Tootie was driving.

If that's what you wanted to call it.

She didn't have her hands at ten o'clock and two. She didn't have a hand at any o'clock. Basically, Tootie drove with one finger on the wheel. Flora's father would have been appalled.

They were in the front seat, all four of them: Tootie, Mary Ann, Flora, and William Spiver. They were speeding down the road. It was alarming and exhilarating to be going so fast.

"So your plan is to effect an exchange?" said William Spiver. "The lamp for the squirrel?"

"Yes," said Flora.

"But—and please correct me if I'm wrong—we have no idea where the squirrel and your mother are."

Flora hated the phrase "correct me if I'm wrong." In her experience, people only said it when they knew they were right.

"Ulysses!" Tootie shouted out her open window. "Ulysses!"

Flora could see the squirrel's name—ULYSSES—flying out of the car and into the night, a single, beautiful word that was immediately swallowed up by the wind and the darkness. Her heart clenched. Why, why, why hadn't she told the squirrel she loved him?

"I hate to be the voice of reason," said William Spiver.

"Don't be, then," said Flora.

"But here we are, speeding down the road. And we are speeding, aren't we, Great-Aunt Tootie? Surely we are exceeding the posted speed limit?"

"I don't see a posted speed limit," said Tootie. She hollered Ulysses's name again.

"In any case," said William Spiver, "it seems that we are going extremely fast. And we are speeding where, exactly? We don't know. We are en route to an unknown destination, calling out the name of a missing squirrel all the while. It doesn't seem one bit rational."

"Well, what's your idea?" said Flora. "What's your plan?"

"We should try to think where your mother would have taken him. We should be logical, methodical, scientific."

"Ulysses!" shouted Tootie.

"Ulysses!" screamed Flora.

"Saying his name won't make him appear," said William Spiver.

But saying William Spiver's name over and over had made *him* appear. This, Flora knew from ***TERRIBLE THINGS CAN HAPPEN TO YOU!***, was magical thinking, or mental causation. According to ***TERRIBLE THINGS!***, it was a dangerous way to think. It was dangerous to allow yourself to believe that what you said directly influenced the universe.

But sometimes it did, didn't it?

Do not hope, Flora thought.

But she couldn't help it. She did hope. She was hoping. She had been hoping all along.

"Ulysses!" she shouted.

The car slowed down.

"What now?" said William Spiver. "Have we spotted something squirrel-related?"

Tootie used a single finger to steer the car to the side of the road.

"Let me guess," said William Spiver as they coasted to a stop. "We've run out of gas."

"We've run out of gas," said Tootie.

"Oh, the symbolism," said William Spiver.

Why, Flora wondered, had she ever thought that William Spiver would be able to help her? Why had she thought of him as her safe port in a storm? Was it because he had held her stupid hand in a stupid dream? Or was it because he never shut up, and she couldn't give up on the idea that he might actually say something at some point that was meaningful, helpful?

Talk about magical thinking.

"Where are we?" Flora said to Tootie.

"I'm not entirely certain," said Tootie.

"Great," said William Spiver. "We're lost. Not that we knew where we were going to begin with."

"We'll have to walk," said Tootie.

"Obviously," said William Spiver, "but walk where?"

CHAPTER SIXTY
He Was Ulysses!

They were in the woods.

He could tell by the smell of pine resin in the trees and the sound of pine needles crunching underfoot. Also, there was the powerful, extremely pervasive scent of raccoon. Raccoons owned the night, and raccoons were truly terrifying creatures — more brutal even than cats.

"This will do," said Flora's mother. She stopped. She put the sack down on the ground. And then she opened it and shone a bright light on Ulysses. He clutched his poem to his chest. He stared into the light as bravely as he could.

"Give me that," said Flora's mother.

She pulled the paper out of his paws. She threw it to the ground. Would she never tire of flinging his words away?

"This is the end of the road, Mr. Squirrel," she said. She put the flashlight on the ground. She picked up a shovel, *the* shovel.

He heard Flora's voice saying, *Remember who you are.*

The squirrel turned and sniffed his tail.

He thought about when Flora had shown him the picture of Alfred T. Slipper in his janitor uniform, and how Alfred had been transformed into the bright light that was Incandesto. The words from the poem that Tootie had recited rose up inside of him.

FLARE UP
LIKE FLAME . . .

AND MAKE BIG
SHADOWS.

HE WASN'T A STONE SQUIRREL.

HE WAS ULYSSES!
ARRRRGGGH!
EEEEEEK!

CHAPTER SIXTY-ONE
I Want to Go Home

You can navigate by the North Star. Supposedly.

Moss grows on the north side of trees. Or so they say.

If you are lost in the woods, you should stay where you are and someone will come and find you. Maybe.

These were the things that Flora had learned about being lost from reading ***TERRIBLE THINGS CAN HAPPEN TO YOU!*** Not that any of it was particularly relevant here. They weren't lost in the woods. They were lost in the universe. Which, according to William Spiver, was expanding. How comforting.

"Ulysses!" shouted Tootie.

"Ulysses!" shouted Flora.

"It's pointless," said William Spiver.

Flora was carrying Mary Ann, and William Spiver was holding on to Tootie's shoulder. Flora hated to agree with William Spiver, but *pointless* seemed like an increasingly appropriate word. Her arms ached from carrying the little shepherdess. Her feet hurt. Her heart hurt.

"Let's see," said Tootie, peering into the darkness. "That's Bricknell Road up there. So we're not truly lost."

"I wish I could see," said William Spiver in a sad voice.

"You *can* see," said Tootie.

"Great-Aunt Tootie," said William Spiver, "I am loath, as

always, to point out the obvious, but I will do it here and now for the sake of clarity. You are not me. You do not exist behind my traumatized eyeballs. I am telling the truth, my truth. I cannot see."

"There's nothing wrong with you, William," said Tootie. "How many times do I have to tell you that?"

"Why did she send me away, then?" said William Spiver. His voice shook.

"You know why she sent you away."

"I do?"

"You can't just push somebody's truck into a lake," said Tootie.

"It was a pond," said William Spiver, "a very small pond. More of a sinkhole, actually."

"You cannot totally submerge somebody's vehicle in a body of water," said Tootie in a very loud voice, "and expect that there aren't going to be severe consequences."

"I did it in a fit of anger," said William Spiver. "I admitted almost immediately that it was a very unfortunate decision."

Tootie shook her head.

"You pushed a truck into a lake?" said Flora. "How did you do that?"

"I released the parking brake, and I put the truck in drive, and I—"

"That's enough," said Tootie. "We don't need a how-to-push-a-truck-into-a-lake lecture."

"Sinkhole," said William Spiver. "It was really a sinkhole."

"Wow," said Flora. "Why did you do it?"

"I was exacting my revenge upon Tyrone," said William Spiver. "My name is William. William. William Spiver. Not Billy. I was Billy one time too many. I cracked. I pushed Tyrone's truck into the sinkhole, and when my mother found out, she was incandescent with rage. I looked upon her rage, and you know what happened then. I was blinded by disbelief and sorrow." He shook his head. "I'm her son. But she made me leave. She sent me away."

Even in the darkness, Flora could see the tears crawling out from underneath William Spiver's dark glasses.

"I want to be called William Spiver," he said. "I want to go home."

Flora felt her heart lurch inside of her.

I want to go home.

It was another one of William Spiver's sad, beautiful sentences.

But will you return?

I came looking for you.

I want to go home.

Flora realized that she wanted to go home, too. She wanted things to be the way they were, before she was banished.

She put Mary Ann down on the ground.

"Give me your hand," she said.

"What?" said William Spiver.

"Give me your hand," said Flora again.

"My hand? Why?"

Flora reached out and grabbed hold of William Spiver's hand, and he held on to her. It was as if he were drowning and she were standing on solid ground. According to ***TERRIBLE THINGS!***, drowning people were desperate, out of their minds with fear. In their panic, they could pull you, the rescuer, under, if you weren't careful.

So Flora held on tightly to William Spiver.

And he held on tightly back.

It was just like her dream. She was holding William Spiver's hand, and he was holding hers.

"Well, if you two are going to walk around holding hands," said Tootie, "I suppose I'll have to be the one who carries this monstrosity of a lamp." She picked up Mary Ann.

Above them, the stars were brilliant, shining brighter than Flora had ever seen them shine.

"I wish my father were here," said William Spiver. He wiped at the tears on his face with his free hand.

An image of Flora's father—hands in his pockets, hat on his head, smiling and saying, "Holy bagumba!" in the voice of Dolores—rose up in Flora's mind.

Her father.

She loved him. She wanted to see his face.

"I know where we should go," said Flora.

CHAPTER SIXTY-TWO
Atop a Giant Donut

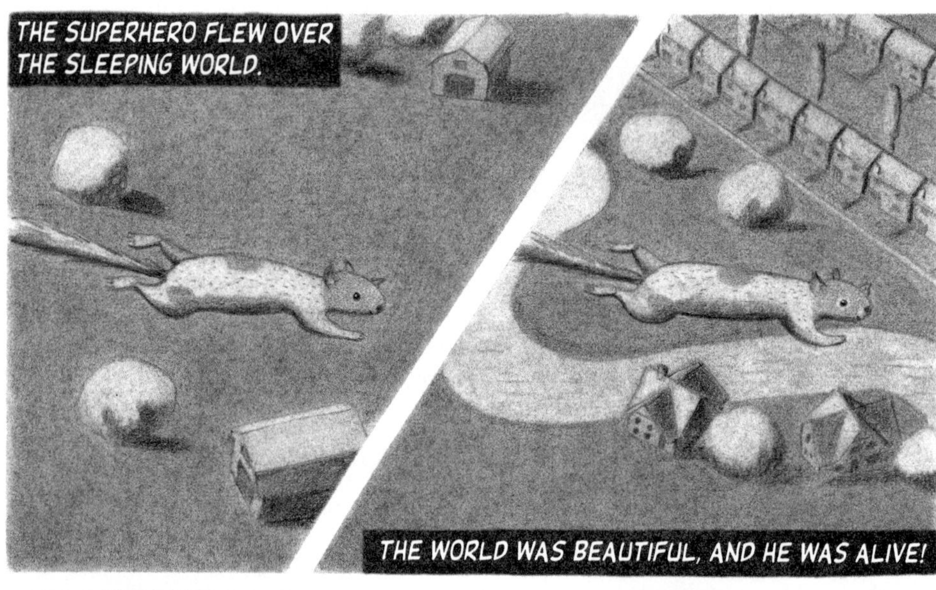

FLORA?

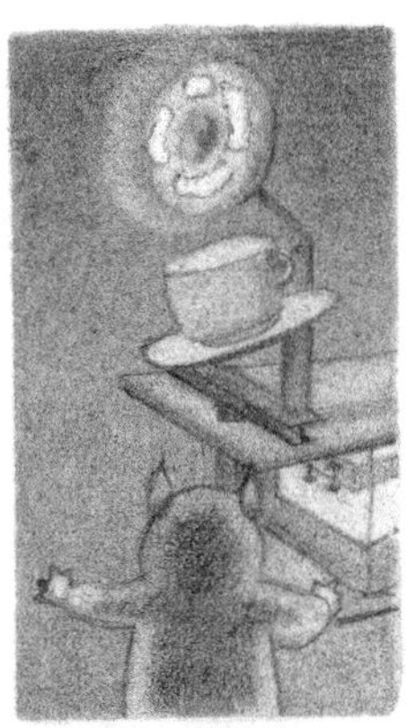

HERE I AM, SITTING ON TOP OF THE GIANT DO-NUT. I WISH FLORA WERE HERE WITH ME.

FLORA?

CHAPTER SIXTY-THREE
Little Fishes

"A squirrel flies in," said Dr. Meescham. "This I did not expect at all. It is what I love about life, that things happen which I do not expect. When I was a girl in Blundermeecen, we left the window open for this very reason, even in the winter. We did it because we believed something wonderful might make its way to us through the open window. Did wonderful things find us? Sometimes yes, sometimes no. But tonight it has happened! Something wonderful!" Dr. Meescham clapped her hands. "A window has been left open. A squirrel flies in the window. The heart of an old woman rejoices!"

Ulysses's heart rejoiced, too. He wasn't lost anymore. Dr. Meescham would help him find Flora.

Also, Dr. Meescham might make him a jelly sandwich.

"Imagine," said Dr. Meescham. "Imagine if I had been sleeping, what I would have missed. But then, always and forever, I have been an insomniac. You know what this is? Insomnia?"

Ulysses shook his head.

"It means I do not sleep. When I was a girl in Blundermeecen, I did not sleep. Who knows why? It could be some existential terror related to the trolls. Or it could be simply because I do not sleep. Sometimes there are no reasons. Often, most of the time, there are no reasons. The world cannot be explained. But I talk too much. I digress. I need to say to you: Why are you here? And where is your Flora Belle?"

Ulysses looked at Dr. Meescham.

He made his eyes very big.

If only there were some way to tell her everything that had happened: Flora's mother saying that life would be easier without her, the universe expanding, William Spiver's banishment, Flora's homesickness, the writing of his poem, the typing of the untrue words, the stone squirrel, the sack, the woods, the shovel . . .

The squirrel was overwhelmed by everything there was to say and his inability to say it.

He looked down at his front paws.

He looked back up at Dr. Meescham.

"Ah," she said, "there is too much to say. You do not know where to begin."

Ulysses nodded.

"Perhaps it would be good to begin with a little snack?"

Ulysses nodded again.

"When the other Dr. Meescham was alive and I could not sleep, do you know what he would do for me? This man would put on his slippers and he would go out into the kitchen and he would fix for me sardines on crackers. You know sardines?"

Ulysses shook his head.

"Little fishes in a can. He would put these little fishes onto crackers for me, and then I would hear him coming back down the hallway, carrying the sardines and humming, returning to me." Dr. Meescham sighed. "Such tenderness. To have someone get out of bed and bring you little fishes and sit with you as you eat them in the dark of night. To hum to you. This is love."

Dr. Meescham wiped at her eyes. She smiled at Ulysses. "So," she said, "I will make for you what my beloved made for me: sardines on crackers. Does this seem like a good thing?"

Ulysses nodded. It seemed like a very good thing.

"We will eat, because this is important, to eat. And then, even though it is the middle of the night, we will go and knock on the door of Mr. George Buckman. And he will open the door to us because he is capacious of heart. And then George Buckman and I will figure out together why you are here and where our Flora Belle is."

Ulysses nodded.

Dr. Meescham went into the kitchen, and the squirrel sat on the windowsill and looked out into the dark world.

Flora was out there somewhere.

He would find her. She would find him. They would find each other. And then he would write her another poem. This one would be about little fishes and humming in the dark of the night.

CHAPTER SIXTY-FOUR
A Miracle

Flora was on the side of the highway.

There were, she had discovered, all kinds of ridiculous things strewn along the side of a road. Shoes, for one thing. And balled-up knee-high stockings. And polyester slacks, baby-blue ones, with a permanent crease. Did people undress as they drove down the road?

There were metal objects: hubcaps, a pair of rusty scissors, a sparkplug. And there were truly inexplicable things. For instance: a plastic banana, glowing a bright and unreal yellow in the dark. That one was interesting. Flora bent down to examine it more closely.

"What are you doing?" said William Spiver. He stopped, too, because she was attached to him and he was attached to her. Which is to say that William Spiver and Flora Belle Buckman were, unbelievably, still holding hands.

"I'm looking at a banana," said Flora.

Tootie was marching ahead of them, holding the little shepherdess out in front of her and shouting Ulysses's name.

William Spiver's hand was getting kind of sweaty. Or maybe it was Flora's hand that was getting sweaty. It was hard to say. William Spiver was still crying (silently) and Ulysses was still missing, and here they were walking along a highway behind an unlit lamp, stopping occasionally to look at knee-high stockings and plastic bananas.

It all must mean something.

But what?

Flora mentally flipped through every issue of *The Illuminated Adventures of the Amazing Incandesto!*, every issue of *TERRIBLE THINGS CAN HAPPEN TO YOU!* and *The Criminal Element Is Among Us*, that she had ever read. She searched for some kind of advice, acknowledgment, the tiniest clue about what to do in this situation.

She came up empty-handed. She was on her own.

She laughed.

"What are you laughing about?" said William Spiver.

Flora laughed louder. William Spiver laughed along with her.

"What's so funny back there?" said Tootie.

"Everything," said Flora.

"Wheeee," said Tootie.

And then they were all laughing. Except for Mary Ann, who couldn't laugh because she was inanimate. But even if she had been capable of laughing, she probably wouldn't have done it. She just wasn't that kind of lamp.

They were all still laughing when the temporarily blind William Spiver stepped on the cord of the little shepherdess and tripped.

And because he refused to let go of Flora's hand (or did she refuse to let go of his?), Flora fell, too. She landed on top of William Spiver.

There was a crunch and then a tinkle.

"Oh, no," said William Spiver, "my glasses! They're broken!"

"For heaven's sake, William," said Tootie. "You don't even need those glasses."

Flora was so close to William Spiver that she could feel his heart beating wildly somewhere inside of him. She thought, *I sure have felt a lot of hearts recently.*

"Wait a minute," said William Spiver. He held his head up. "Everyone be quiet. Shhh. What are those tiny pinpricks of light?"

Flora looked where William Spiver was looking. "Those are stars, William Spiver."

"I can see the stars! I can see! Great-Aunt Tootie! Flora Belle, I can see!"

"It's a miracle," said Tootie.

"Or something," said Flora.

CHAPTER SIXTY-FIVE
Open the Door

The hallway of the Blixen Arms emitted the same green gloomy light no matter the time of day or night.

"Watch out for the cat," said Flora.

"The infamous Mr. Klaus," said William Spiver. He looked around. He was smiling. "The cat who was defeated by a superhero squirrel. I will certainly keep an eye out for him. And I hate to sound like a broken record, but may I just say again what a delight it is to *see*? Talk about being born anew. Nothing, nothing, will ever again escape my notice."

"Goody," said Tootie.

"I'm not kidding," said Flora. "Mr. Klaus could be anywhere."

"Yes," said William Spiver. "My eyes are open. They are open, indeed."

"Knock again," said Tootie.

Flora knocked again.

Where could her father be in the middle of the night? Had someone kidnapped him, too? Was it kidnapping if it was an adult? Or was that adult-napping? George Buckman–napping?

And then she heard her father laugh.

But the laugh wasn't coming from his apartment. It was coming from apartment 267.

"Dr. Meescham!" said Flora.

"Who?" said William Spiver.

"Dr. Meescham. Knock on that door, quick," said Flora to William Spiver. She pointed, and William Spiver raised his hand to knock just as the door to Dr. Meescham's apartment swung wide.

"Flora Belle," said Dr. Meescham. "My little flower, our beloved." She was smiling very big. Her teeth were glowing. Ulysses was sitting on her shoulder.

Behind Ulysses and Dr. Meescham was Flora's father. He was wearing his pajamas. His hat was on his head.

"George Buckman," said her father, slowly raising his hat to them all. "How do you do?"

"Ulysses?" said Flora.

She said his name like a question.

And he answered her.

He flew to her; his small, warm, hopeful body hit her with a thud that almost knocked her off her feet. She wrapped her arms, her hands, her self around him.

"Ulysses," she said. "I love you."

"So much happiness!" said Dr. Meescham. "This is how it was when I was a girl in Blundermeecen. Like this. Always opening the door in the middle of the night and finding the face of someone you wanted to see. Well, not always. Sometimes it was the face of someone you did not want to see.

"But always, always in Blundermeecen, you opened the

door because you could not stop hoping that on the other side of it would be the face of someone you loved." Dr. Meescham looked at William Spiver and then at Tootie. She smiled. "And maybe, too, the face of someone you did not yet know but might come to love."

"Tootie Tickham," said Tootie. "It's a pleasure to meet you. And this is my nephew, William. I would shake your hand, but as you can see I am in charge of this lamp."

"Actually," said William Spiver, "I am her great-nephew. And my name is William Spiver. And I realize that it is early in our acquaintance for me to be revealing such astonishing and deeply personal information, but I must tell you that I was temporarily blind and now I can see! Also, I feel compelled to say that your face is beautiful to me. In fact, every face is beautiful to me." He turned. "Your face, Flora Belle, is particularly beautiful. Even the sepulchral gloom of this hallway cannot dim your loveliness."

"Sepulchral gloom?" said Flora.

"That's because she is a flower," said Flora's father, "my lovely flower."

Flora felt herself blushing.

"It is a lovely face, the face of Flora Belle Buckman," said Dr. Meescham. "It is truly beautiful. But you have all stood long enough outside; you must come inside now. Come."

CHAPTER SIXTY-SIX
Will You Please, Please Shut Up, William Spiver?

"So," said Dr. Meescham, "we have been speaking with Ulysses. We have been working to understand his story. From what we have put together so far, it involves a shovel and a sack. And the woods. And a poem."

"And a giant donut," said Flora's father.

Ulysses, sitting on Flora's shoulder, nodded vigorously. A distinctly fishy smell emanated from his whiskers.

Flora turned to him. "Where's my mother?" she said.

Ulysses shook his head.

"Pop?" said Flora. "Where's Mom?"

"I'm not certain," said her father. He adjusted his hat. He tried to put his hands in his pockets, and then he realized he was wearing pajamas and had no pockets. He laughed. "Holy bagumba," he said softly.

"We need a typewriter," said Flora.

Ulysses nodded.

"We need a typewriter so that we can get to the truth," said Flora.

"The truth," said William Spiver, "is a slippery thing. I doubt that you will ever get to *The* Truth. You may get to a version of the truth. But *The* Truth? I doubt it very seriously."

"Will you please, please shut up, William Spiver?" said Flora.

"Shhh," said Dr. Meescham. "Calm, calm. You should maybe sit and eat a sardine."

"I don't want a sardine," said Flora. "I want to know what happened. I want to know where my mother is."

Just as she said these words, there was a bang, which was followed by a long, bone-chilling yowl, which was, in turn, followed by a very loud scream.

"What was that?" said William Spiver.

"That's Mr. Klaus," said Flora. "He's attacking someone."

There was another scream, and then came the words, "George, George!"

"Uh-oh," said Flora's father. "It's Phyllis."

"Mom," said Flora.

Ulysses tensed. He dug his claws into Flora's shoulder.

Flora looked at him.

He nodded.

And then Flora's father was running out the door, and Flora was behind him and William Spiver was behind her. Another of her mother's screams echoed down the hallway. "George, George," she shouted, "please tell me that my baby is here!"

Flora turned and said to Tootie, "Bring the lamp! She's worried about Mary Ann."

There was another scream.

IT WAS TIME (AGAIN) FOR THE SQUIRREL TO VANQUISH A VILLAIN!
IT WAS TIME FOR ULYSSES TO RESCUE HIS ARCH-NEMESIS!

WHO WILL PREVAIL?

WHO WILL BE VANQUISHED?

Me? thought Flora.

"She's here," said Flora's father.

Flora's mother started to cry.

"Everyone needs to calm down," said Tootie. "I've got it." She waded into the fray and whacked Mr. Klaus over the head with Mary Ann.

The cat fell to the ground, and the little shepherdess, as if she were astonished by her own act of violence, crumbled. Her face—her beautiful, perfect pink face—broke. There was a tinkle and a crash as the pieces of Mary Ann's head hit the floor.

"Oops," said Tootie. "I broke her."

"Uh-oh," said Flora.

But her mother wasn't looking at the lamp or what was left of the lamp. She was looking at Flora.

"Flora," her mother said. "Flora. I went home, and you weren't there. I was terrified."

"Here she is," said William Spiver. He gave Flora a gentle shove toward her mother.

"Here I am," said Flora.

Her mother stepped over the pieces of the broken little shepherdess. She took Flora in her arms.

"My baby," said her mother.

"Me?" said Flora.

"You," said her mother.

CHAPTER SIXTY-SEVEN
The Horsehair Sofa

Flora's mother was sitting on the horsehair sofa. Flora's father was sitting next to her. He was holding her hand. Or she was holding his. In any case, her mother and her father were holding on to each other.

Dr. Meescham was putting alcohol on Flora's mother's bites and scratches. "Ouch, ouch, oooooh," said Flora's mother.

"Come," said Dr. Meescham to Flora. She patted the horsehair sofa. "Sit down. Here. Beside your mother."

Flora sat down on the couch and immediately started to slide off it. Was there a trick to sitting on the horsehair sofa? Because she certainly hadn't mastered it.

And then William Spiver sat down beside her so that she was wedged in between her mother and him.

Flora stopped sliding.

"And I went up to your room," said Flora's mother. "I climbed the stairs to your room, and you weren't there."

"I was out looking for Ulysses," said Flora. "I thought you had kidnapped him."

"It's true," confessed her mother. "I did."

Ulysses, sitting on Flora's shoulder, nodded. His whiskers brushed her cheek.

"I wanted to make things right somehow. I wanted to make things normal," said Flora's mother.

"Normalcy is an illusion, of course," said William Spiver. "There is no normal."

"Hush up, William," said Tootie.

"And when I returned and you weren't there . . ." said Flora's mother. She started to cry again. "I don't care about normal. I just wanted you back. I needed to find you."

"And here she is, Mrs. Buckman," said William Spiver in a very gentle voice.

Here I am, thought Flora. *And my mother loves me. Holy bagumba.*

And then she thought, *Oh, no, I'm going to cry.*

And she did cry. Big, fat tears rolled down her face and landed on the horsehair sofa and trembled there for a second before they rolled off.

"You see?" said Dr. Meescham. She smiled at Flora. "I told you. This is how it is with this sofa."

"Mrs. Buckman," said William Spiver, "what is that that you are holding in your hand? What is that piece of paper?"

"It's a poem," said Flora's mother, "by Ulysses. It's for Flora."

"Look at this!" said Tootie.

They all turned and looked at Tootie. She was standing by the headless Mary Ann, who was plugged in and shining. "It still works. Isn't that something?"

"Why don't you read the poem, Phyllis?" said Flora's father.

"Oh, goody," said Tootie, "a poetry reading."

"It's a squirrel poem," said Flora's mother. "But it's a good one."

Ulysses puffed out his chest.

"'Words for Flora,'" her mother said. "That's the title."

"I like that title," said William Spiver.

He took hold of Flora's hand. He squeezed it.

"Don't squeeze my hand," said Flora.

But she held on tightly to William Spiver, and she listened as her mother read the poem that Ulysses had written.

CHAPTER SIXTY-EIGHT
The End (or Something)

This poem was just the beginning, of course.

There would be more.

He needed to write about how they always, always answered the door in Blundermeecen. He needed to write about the saving of Phyllis Buckman from Mr. Klaus. He needed to write about Mary Ann's broken, still-shining self. And little fishes.

He needed to write a poem about little fishes.

Also, he wanted to write about things that hadn't happened yet. For instance, he wanted to write a poem where William Spiver's mother called and asked for him to come home. And a poem where the other Dr. Meescham came and visited this Dr. Meescham and sat beside her and hummed to her and watched her sleep. And maybe there would be a poem about a horsehair sofa. And one about a vacuum cleaner.

He would write and write. He would make wonderful things happen. Some of it would be true. All of it would be true.

Most of it would be true.

Ulysses looked out the window and saw the sun glowing on the horizon. Soon it would be time to eat.

A wonderful thought occurred to the squirrel.

Maybe there would be donuts, giant donuts, for breakfast.

EPILOGUE

Squirrel Poetry

Words for Flora

Nothing
would be
easier without
you,
because you
are
everything,
all of it—
sprinkles, quarks, giant
donuts, eggs sunny-side up—
you
are the ever-expanding
universe
to me.